Selected Stories by
SIR ARTHUR CONAN DOYLE

Books in this Series:

Selected Stories by
SIR ARTHUR CONAN DOYLE

RUPA

Published by
Rupa Publications India Pvt. Ltd 2014
7/16, Ansari Road, Daryaganj
New Delhi 110002

Sales Centres:
Allahabad Bengaluru Chennai
Hyderabad Jaipur Kathmandu
Kolkata Mumbai

Selection and Introduction copyright © Terry O'Brien 2014

ISBN: 978-81-291-3142-3

First impression 2014

10 9 8 7 6 5 4 3 2 1

Printed at Shree Maitrey Printech Pvt. Ltd., Noida

CONTENTS

INTRODUCTION

Sir Arthur Ignatius Conan Doyle DL (22 May 1859—7 July 1930) was a Scottish physician and writer who is most noted for his fictional stories about the detective Sherlock Holmes, which are generally considered milestones in the field of crime fiction.

56 short Sherlock Holmes stories were written by Sir Arthur Conan Doyle. Incidentally, Doyle was not knighted for his literary work; it was for his services to the British Crown that Edward VII knighted him as a defender of the British activities in the South African War (Boer War) in 1902.

- A man's face appears in a second-floor window to his wife as he lets out a cry, and then mysteriously vanishes. It is up to Sherlock Holmes and his trusty companion Dr. Watson to find out what has happened to him, in 'The Man With The Twisted Lip'.
- A woman appeals helplessly to Sherlock Holmes about the case of her missing fiance, which leads to quite an ingenius albeit elementary revelation for the detective—in 'A Case Of Identity'.
- A speckled band is sighted by a woman right before she dies; two years later, her sister seems to facing a similar horrific death—until Sherlock Holmes steps in to get to the bottom of a most brutal crime in 'The Adventure of the Speckled band.'
- 'The Adventure Of The Yellow Face' begins with a seemingly

straightforward problem brought to Holmes and Watson, about a husband uncertain about his wife's secret, but then goes on to reveal something completely unexpected.

- A young clerk consult Holmes with his suspicions concerning a company that has hired him, and thus begins the riveting tale of 'The Adventure of the Stockbroker's Clerk'.

- The colonel is dead, apparently by violence, and his wife, who was the only one in the room with him, is the prime suspect. But there is more to it than meets the eye, as Holmes and Watson find out in 'The Adventure of the Crooked Man'.

- 'The Adventure of the "Gloria Scott"' is a throwback to Sherlock Holmes's very first case in his university days. It tells of an intriguing chain of events that are revealed after Holmes spends a month with his only friend from college, at his father's estate in Norfolk.

Sherlock Holmes still lives today: his relevance lies in his infinite variety. With more than seventy actors having played Sherlock Holmes in two hundred films and television series, the fictitious detective has been reinvented many times. The interpretations of Arthur Conan Doyle's character have never been more popular than they are today.

1

THE MAN WITH THE TWISTED LIP

Isa Whitney, brother of the late Elias Whitney, D.D., Principal of the Theological College of St. George's, was much addicted to opium. The habit grew upon him, as I understand, from some foolish freak when he was at college; for having read De Quincey's description of his dreams and sensations, he had drenched his tobacco with laudanum in an attempt to produce the same effects. He found, as so many more have done, that the practice is easier to attain than to get rid of, and for many years he continued to be a slave to the drug, an object of mingled horror and pity to his friends and relatives. I can see him now, with yellow, pasty face, drooping lids, and pin-point pupils, all huddled in a chair, the wreck and ruin of a noble man.

One night—it was in June, '89—there came a ring to my bell, about the hour when a man gives his first yawn and glances at the clock. I sat up in my chair, and my wife laid her needle-work down in her lap and made a little face of disappointment.

'A patient!' said she. 'You'll have to go out.'

I groaned, for I was newly come back from a weary day.

We heard the door open, a few hurried words, and then quick steps upon the linoleum. Our own door flew open, and a lady, clad in some dark-coloured stuff, with a black veil, entered the room.

'You will excuse my calling so late,' she began, and then,

suddenly losing her self-control, she ran forward, threw her arms about my wife's neck, and sobbed upon her shoulder. 'Oh, I'm in such trouble!' she cried; 'I do so want a little help.'

'Why,' said my wife, pulling up her veil, 'it is Kate Whitney. How you startled me, Kate! I had not an idea who you were when you came in.'

'I didn't know what to do, so l came straight to you.' That was always the way. Folk who were in grief came to my wife like birds to a light-house.

'It was very sweet of you to come. Now, you must have some wine and water, and sit here comfortably and tell us all about it. Or should you rather that I sent James off to bed?'

'Oh, no, no! I want the doctor's advice and help, too. It's about Isa. He has not been home for two days. I am so frightened about him!'

It was not the first time that she had spoken to us of her husband's trouble, to me as a doctor, to my wife as an old friend and school companion. We soothed and comforted her by such words as we could find. Did she know where her husband was? Was it possible that we could bring him back to her?

It seems that it was. She had the surest information that of late he had, when the fit was on him, made use of an opium den in the farthest east of the City. Hitherto his orgies had always been confined to one day, and he had come back, twitching and shattered, in the evening. But now the spell had been upon him eight-and-forty hours, and he lay there, doubtless among the dregs of the docks, breathing in the poison or sleeping off the effects. There he was to be found, she was sure of it, at the Bar of Gold, in Upper Swandam Lane. But what was she to do? How could she, a young and timid woman, make her way into such a place and pluck her husband out from among the ruffians who surrounded him?

There was the case, and of course there was but one way out of it. Might I not escort her to this place? And then, as a second thought, why should she come at all? I was Isa Whitney's medical adviser, and as such I had influence over him. I could manage it better if I were alone. I promised her on my word that I would send him home in a cab within two hours if he were indeed at the address which she had given me. And so in ten minutes I had left my armchair and cheery sitting-room behind me, and was speeding eastward in a hansom on a strange errand, as it seemed to me at the time, though the future only could show how strange it was to be.

But there was no great difficulty in the first stage of my adventure. Upper Swandam Lane is a vile alley lurking behind the high wharves which line the north side of the river to the east of London Bridge. Between a slop-shop and a gin-shop, approached by a steep flight of steps leading down to a black gap like the mouth of a cave, I found the den of which I was in search. Ordering my cab to wait, I passed down the steps, worn hollow in the centre by the ceaseless tread of drunken feet; and by the light of a flickering oil-lamp above the door, I found the latch and made my way into a long, low room, thick and heavy with the brown opium smoke, and terraced with wooden berths, like the forecastle of an emigrant ship.

Through the gloom one could dimly catch a glimpse of bodies lying in strange fantastic poses, bowed shoulders, bent knees, heads thrown back, and chins pointing upward, with here and there a dark, lack-lustre eye turned upon the newcomer. Out of the black shadows there glimmered little red circles of light, now bright, now faint, as the burning poison waxed or waned in the bowls of the metal pipes. The most lay silent, but some muttered to themselves, and others talked together in a strange, low, monotonous voice, their conversation coming in gushes, and then suddenly tailing off into silence, each mumbling out his own thoughts and paying little heed to the words of his neighbour. At the farther end was a small brazier of burning charcoal, beside which on a three-legged wooden stool there sat a tall, thin old man, with his jaw resting upon his two fists, and his elbows upon his knees, staring into the fire.

As I entered, a sallow Malay attendant had hurried up with a pipe for me and a supply of the drug, beckoning me to an empty berth.

'Thank you. I have not come to stay,' said I. 'There is a friend of mine here, Mr Isa Whitney, and I wish to speak with him.'

There was a movement and an exclamation from my right, and peering through the gloom I saw Whitney, pale, haggard, and unkempt, staring out at me.

'My God! It's Watson,' said he. He was in a pitiable state of reaction, with every nerve in a twitter. 'I say, Watson, what o'clock is it?'

'Nearly eleven.'

'Of what day?'

'Of Friday, June 19th.'

'Good heavens! I thought it was Wednesday. It is Wednesday. What d'you want to frighten the chap for?' He sank his face onto his arms and began to sob in a high treble key.

'I tell you that it is Friday, man. Your wife has been waiting this two days for you. You should be ashamed of yourself!'

'So I am. But you've got mixed, Watson, for I have only been here a few hours, three pipes, four pipes—I forget how many. But I'll go home with you. I wouldn't frighten Kate—poor little Kate. Give me your hand! Have you a cab?'

'Yes, I have one waiting.'

'Then I shall go in it. But I must owe something. Find what I owe, Watson. I am all off colour. I can do nothing for myself.'

I walked down the narrow passage between the double row of sleepers, holding my breath to keep out the vile, stupefying fumes of the drug, and looking about for the manager. As I passed the tall man who sat by the brazier, I felt a sudden pluck at my skirt, and a low voice whispered, 'Walk past me, and then look back at me.' The words fell quite distinctly upon my ear. I glanced down. They could only have come from the old man at my side, and yet he sat now as absorbed as ever, very thin, very wrinkled, bent with age, an opium pipe dangling down from between his knees, as though it had dropped in sheer lassitude from his fingers. I took two steps forward and looked back. It took all my self-control to prevent me from breaking out into a cry of astonishment. He had turned his back so that none could see him but I. His form had filled out, his wrinkles were gone, the dull eyes had regained their fire, and there, sitting by the fire and grinning at my surprise, was none other than Sherlock Holmes. He made a slight motion to me to approach him, and instantly, as he turned his face half round to the company once more, subsided into a doddering, loose-lipped senility.

'Holmes!' I whispered, 'what on earth are you doing in this den?'

'As low as you can,' he answered; 'I have excellent ears. If you would have the great kindness to get rid of that sottish friend of yours I should be exceedingly glad to have a little talk with you.'

'I have a cab outside.'

'Then pray send him home in it. You may safely trust him, for he appears to be too limp to get into any mischief. I should recommend you also to send a note by the cabman to your wife to say that you have thrown in your lot with me. If you will wait outside, I shall be with you in five minutes.'

It was difficult to refuse any of Sherlock Holmes's requests, for they were always so exceedingly definite, and put forward with such a quiet air of mastery. I felt, however, that when Whitney was once confined in the cab my mission was practically accomplished; and for the rest, I could not wish anything better than to be associated with my friend in one of those singular adventures which were the normal condition of his existence. In a few minutes I had written my note, paid Whitney's bill, led him out to the cab, and seen him driven through the darkness. In a very short time, a decrepit figure had emerged from the opium den, and I was walking down the street with Sherlock Holmes. For two streets he shuffled along with a bent back and an uncertain foot. Then, glancing quickly round, he straightened himself out and burst into a hearty fit of laughter.

'I suppose, Watson,' said he, 'that you imagine that I have added opium-smoking to cocaine injections, and all the other little weaknesses on which you have favoured me with your medical views.'

'I was certainly surprised to find you there.'

'But not more so than I to find you.'

'I came to find a friend.'

'And I to find an enemy.'

'An enemy?'

'Yes; one of my natural enemies, or, shall I say, my natural prey. Briefly, Watson, I am in the midst of a very remarkable inquiry, and I have hoped to find a clue in the incoherent ramblings of these sots, as I have done before now. Had I been recognized in that den my life would not have been worth an hour's purchase; for I have used it before now for my own purposes, and the rascally lascar who runs it has sworn to have vengeance upon me. There is a trap-door at the back of that building, near the corner of Paul's Wharf, which could tell some strange tales of what has passed through it upon the moonless nights.'

'What! You do not mean bodies?'

'Ay, bodies, Watson. We should be rich men if we had 1000 pounds for every poor devil who has been done to death in that den. It is the vilest murder-trap on the whole riverside, and I fear that Neville St. Clair has entered it never to leave it more. But our trap should be here.' He put his two forefingers between his teeth and whistled shrilly—a signal which was answered by a similar whistle from the distance, followed shortly by the rattle of wheels and the clink of horses' hoofs.

'Now, Watson,' said Holmes, as a tall dog-cart dashed up through the gloom, throwing out two golden tunnels of yellow light from its side lanterns. 'You'll come with me, won't you?'

'If I can be of use.'

'Oh, a trusty comrade is always of use; and a chronicler still more so. My room at The Cedars is a double-bedded one.'

'The Cedars?'

'Yes; that is Mr St. Clair's house. I am staying there while I conduct the inquiry.'

'Where is it, then?'

'Near Lee, in Kent. We have a seven-mile drive before us.'

'But I am all in the dark.'

'Of course you are. You'll know all about it presently. Jump up here. All right, John; we shall not need you. Here's half a crown. Look out for me tomorrow, about eleven. Give her her head. So long, then!'

He flicked the horse with his whip, and we dashed away through the endless succession of sombre and deserted streets, which widened gradually, until we were flying across a broad balustraded bridge, with the murky river flowing sluggishly beneath us. Beyond lay another dull wilderness of bricks and mortar, its silence broken only by the heavy, regular footfall of the policeman, or the songs and shouts of some belated party of revellers. A dull wrack was drifting slowly across the sky, and a star or two twinkled dimly here and there through the rifts of the clouds. Holmes drove in silence, with his head sunk upon his breast, and the air of a man who is lost in thought, while I sat beside him, curious to learn what this new quest might be which seemed to tax his powers so sorely, and yet afraid to break in upon the current of his thoughts. We had driven several miles, and were beginning to get to the fringe of the belt of suburban villas, when he shook himself, shrugged his shoulders, and lit up his pipe with the air of a man who has satisfied himself that he is acting for the best.

'You have a grand gift of silence, Watson,' said he. 'It makes you quite invaluable as a companion. 'Pon my word, it is a great thing for me to have someone to talk to, for my own thoughts are not over-pleasant. I was wondering what I should say to this dear little woman tonight when she meets me at the door.'

'You forget that I know nothing about it.'

'I shall just have time to tell you the facts of the case before we get to Lee. It seems absurdly simple, and yet, somehow I can get nothing to go upon. There's plenty of thread, no doubt, but I can't get the end of it into my hand. Now, I'll state the case clearly and concisely to you, Watson, and maybe you can see a spark where all is dark to me.'

'Proceed, then.'

'Some years ago—to be definite, in May, 1884—there came to Lee a gentleman, Neville St. Clair by name, who appeared to have plenty of money. He took a large villa, laid out the grounds very nicely, and lived generally in good style. By degrees he made friends in the neighbourhood, and in 1887 he married the daughter of a local brewer, by whom he now has two children. He had no occupation, but was interested in several companies and went into town as a rule in the morning, returning by the 5.14 from Cannon Street every night. Mr St. Clair is now thirty-seven years of age, is a man of temperate habits, a good husband, a very affectionate father, and a man who is popular with all who know him. I may add that his whole debts at the present moment, as far as we have been able to ascertain amount to £88.10, while he has £220 standing to his credit in the Capital and Counties Bank. There is no reason, therefore, to think that money troubles have been weighing upon his mind.

'Last Monday, Mr Neville St. Clair went into town rather

earlier than usual, remarking before he started that he had two important commissions to perform, and that he would bring his little boy home a box of bricks. Now, by the merest chance, his wife received a telegram upon this same Monday, very shortly after his departure, to the effect that a small parcel of considerable value which she had been expecting was waiting for her at the offices of the Aberdeen Shipping Company. Now, if you are well up in your London, you will know that the office of the company is in Fresno Street, which branches out of Upper Swandam Lane, where you found me tonight. Mrs St. Clair had her lunch, started for the City, did some shopping, proceeded to the company's office, got her packet, and found herself at exactly 4.35 walking through Swandam Lane on her way back to the station. Have you followed me so far?'

'It is very clear.'

'If you remember, Monday was an exceedingly hot day, and Mrs St. Clair walked slowly, glancing about in the hope of seeing a cab, as she did not like the neighbourhood in which she found herself. While she was walking in this way down Swandam Lane, she suddenly heard an ejaculation or cry, and was struck cold to see her husband looking down at her and, as it seemed to her, beckoning to her from a second-floor window. The window was open, and she distinctly saw his face, which she describes as being terribly agitated. He waved his hands frantically to her, and then vanished from the window so suddenly that it seemed to her that he had been plucked back by some irresistible force from behind. One singular point which struck her quick feminine eye was that although he wore some dark coat, such as he had started to town in, he had on neither collar nor necktie.

'Convinced that something was amiss with him, she rushed down the steps—for the house was none other than the opium den, in which you found me tonight—and running through the front room she attempted to ascend the stairs which led to the first floor. At the foot of the stairs, however, she met this lascar scoundrel of whom I have spoken, who thrust her back and, aided by a Dane, who acts as assistant there, pushed her out into the street. Filled with the most maddening doubts and fears, she rushed down the lane and, by rare good fortune, met in Fresno Street a number of constables with an inspector, all on their way to their beat. The inspector and two men accompanied her back, and in spite of the continued resistance of the proprietor, they made their way to the room in which Mr St. Clair had last been seen. There was no sign of him there. In fact, in the whole of that floor there was no one to be found save a crippled wretch of hideous aspect, who, it seems, made his home there. Both he and the lascar stoutly swore that no one else had been in the front room during the afternoon. So determined was their denial that the inspector was staggered, and had almost come to believe that Mrs St. Clair had been deluded when, with a cry, she sprang at a small deal box which lay upon the table and tore the lid from it. Out there fell a cascade of children's bricks. It was the toy which he had promised to bring home.

'This discovery, and the evident confusion which the cripple showed, made the inspector realize that the matter was serious. The rooms were carefully examined, and results all pointed to an abominable crime. The front room was plainly furnished as a sitting-room and led into a small bedroom, which looked out upon the back of one of the wharves. Between the wharf and the bedroom window is a narrow strip, which is dry at low tide but is covered at high tide with at least four and a half feet of water. The bedroom window was a broad one and opened from below. On examination, traces of blood were to be seen upon the windowsill, and several scattered drops were visible upon the wooden floor of the bedroom. Thrust away behind a curtain in the front room were all the clothes of Mr Neville St. Clair, with the exception of his coat. His boots, his socks, his hat, and his watch—all were there. There were no signs of violence upon any of these garments, and there were no other traces of Mr Neville St. Clair. Out of the window he must apparently have gone for no other exit could be discovered, and the ominous bloodstains upon the sill gave little promise that he could save himself by swimming, for the tide was at its very highest at the moment of the tragedy.

'And now as to the villains who seemed to be immediately implicated in the matter. The lascar was known to be a man of the vilest antecedents, but as, by Mrs St. Clair's story, he was known to have been at the foot of the stair within a very few seconds of her husband's appearance at the window, he could hardly have been more than an accessory to the crime. His defence was one of absolute ignorance, and he protested that he had no knowledge as to the doings of Hugh Boone, his lodger, and that he could not account in any way for the presence of the missing gentleman's clothes.

'So much for the lascar manager. Now for the sinister cripple who lives upon the second floor of the opium den, and who was certainly the last human being whose eyes rested upon Neville St. Clair. His name is Hugh Boone, and his hideous face is one which is familiar to every man who goes much to the City. He is a professional beggar, though in order to avoid the police regulations he pretends to a small trade in wax vestas. Some little distance down Threadneedle Street, upon the left-hand side, there is, as you may have remarked, a small angle in the wall. Here it is that this creature takes his daily seat, cross-legged with his tiny stock of matches on his lap, and as he is a piteous spectacle a small rain of charity descends into the greasy leather cap which lies upon the pavement beside him. I have watched the fellow more than once before ever I thought of making his professional acquaintance, and I have been surprised at the harvest which he has reaped in a short time. His appearance, you see, is so remarkable that no one can pass him without observing him. A shock of orange hair, a pale face disfigured by a horrible scar, which, by its contraction, has turned up the outer edge of his upper lip, a bulldog chin, and a pair of very penetrating dark eyes, which present a singular contrast to the colour of his hair, all mark him out from amid the common crowd of mendicants and so, too, does his wit, for he is ever ready with a reply to any piece of chaff which may be thrown at him by the passers-by. This is the man whom we now learn to have been the lodger at the opium den, and to have been the last man to see the gentleman of whom we are in quest.'

'But a cripple!' said I. 'What could he have done singlehanded against a man in the prime of life?'

'He is a cripple in the sense that he walks with a limp; but in other respects he appears to be a powerful and well-nurtured man. Surely your medical experience would tell you, Watson, that weakness in one limb is often compensated for by exceptional strength in the others.'

'Pray continue your narrative.'

'Mrs St. Clair had fainted at the sight of the blood upon the window, and she was escorted home in a cab by the police, as her presence could be of no help to them in their investigations. Inspector Barton, who had charge of the case, made a very careful examination of the premises, but without finding anything which threw any light upon the matter. One mistake had been made in not arresting Boone instantly, as he was allowed some few minutes during which he might have communicated with his friend the lascar, but this fault was soon remedied, and he was seized and searched, without anything being found which could incriminate him. There were, it is true, some blood-stains upon his right shirtsleeve, but he pointed to his ring-finger, which had been cut near the nail, and explained that the bleeding came from there, adding that he had been to the window not long before, and that the stains which had been observed there came doubtless from the same source. He denied strenuously having ever seen Mr Neville

St. Clair and swore that the presence of the clothes in his room was as much a mystery to him as to the police. As to Mrs St. Clair's assertion that she had actually seen her husband at the window, he declared that she must have been either mad or dreaming. He was removed, loudly protesting, to the policestation, while the inspector remained upon the premises in the hope that the ebbing tide might afford some fresh clue.

'And it did, though they hardly found upon the mud-bank what they had feared to find. It was Neville St. Clair's coat, and not Neville St. Clair, which lay uncovered as the tide receded. And what do you think they found in the pockets?'

'I cannot imagine.'

'No, I don't think you would guess. Every pocket stuffed with pennies and half-pennies—421 pennies and 270 half-pennies. It was no wonder that it had not been swept away by the tide. But a human body is a different matter. There is a fierce eddy between the wharf and the house. It seemed likely enough that the weighted coat had remained when the stripped body had been sucked away into the river.'

'But I understand that all the other clothes were found in the room. Would the body be dressed in a coat alone?'

'No, sir, but the facts might be met speciously enough. Suppose that this man Boone had thrust Neville St. Clair through the window, there is no human eye which could have seen the deed. What would he do then? It would of course instantly strike him that he must get rid of the tell-tale garments. He would seize the coat, then, and be in the act of throwing it out, when it would occur to him that it would swim and not sink. He has little time, for he has heard the scuffle downstairs when the wife tried to force her way up, and perhaps he has already heard from his lascar confederate that the police are hurrying up the street. There is not an instant to be lost. He rushes to some secret hoard, where he has accumulated the fruits of his beggary, and he stuffs all the coins upon which he can lay his hands into the pockets to make sure of the coat's sinking. He throws it out, and would have done the same with the other garments had not he heard the rush of steps below, and only just had time to close the window when the police appeared.'

'It certainly sounds feasible.'

'Well, we will take it as a working hypothesis for want of a better. Boone, as I have told you, was arrested and taken to the station, but it could not be shown that there had ever before been anything against him. He had for years been known as a professional beggar, but his life appeared to have been a very quiet and innocent one. There the matter stands at present, and the questions which have to be solved—what Neville St. Clair was doing in the opium den, what happened to him when there, where is he now, and what Hugh Boone had to do with his disappearance—are all as far from a solution as ever. I confess that I cannot recall any case within my experience which looked at the first glance so simple and yet which presented such difficulties.'

While Sherlock Holmes had been detailing this singular series of events, we had been whirling through the outskirts of the great town until the last straggling houses had been left behind, and we rattled along with a country hedge upon either side of us. Just as he finished, however, we drove through two scattered villages, where a few lights still glimmered in the windows.

'We are on the outskirts of Lee,' said my companion. 'We have touched on three English counties in our short drive, starting in Middlesex, passing over an angle of Surrey, and ending in Kent. See that light among the trees? That is The Cedars, and beside that lamp sits a woman whose anxious ears have already, I have little doubt, caught the clink of our horse's feet.'

'But why are you not conducting the case from Baker Street?' I asked.

'Because there are many inquiries which must be made out

here. Mrs St. Clair has most kindly put two rooms at my disposal, and you may rest assured that she will have nothing but a welcome for my friend and colleague. I hate to meet her, Watson, when I have no news of her husband. Here we are. Whoa, there, whoa!'

We had pulled up in front of a large villa which stood within its own grounds. A stable-boy had run out to the horse's head, and springing down I followed Holmes up the small, winding gravel-drive which led to the house. As we approached, the door flew open, and a little blonde woman stood in the opening, clad in some sort of light mousseline de soie, with a touch of fluffy pink chiffon at her neck and wrists. She stood with her figure outlined against the flood of light, one hand upon the door, one half-raised in her eagerness, her body slightly bent, her head and face protruded, with eager eyes and parted lips, a standing question.

'Well?' she cried, 'Well?' And then, seeing that there were two of us, she gave a cry of hope which sank into a groan as she saw that my companion shook his head and shrugged his shoulders.

'No good news?'

'None.'

'No bad?'

'No.'

'Thank God for that. But come in. You must be weary, for you have had a long day.'

'This is my friend, Dr. Watson. He has been of most vital use to me in several of my cases, and a lucky chance has made it possible for me to bring him out and associate him with this investigation.'

'I am delighted to see you,' said she, pressing my hand warmly. 'You will, I am sure, forgive anything that may be wanting in our arrangements, when you consider the blow which has come so suddenly upon us.'

'My dear madam,' said I, 'I am an old campaigner, and if I were not I can very well see that no apology is needed. If I can be of any assistance, either to you or to my friend here, I shall be indeed happy.'

'Now, Mr Sherlock Holmes,' said the lady as we entered a well-lit dining room, upon the table of which a cold supper had been laid out, 'I should very much like to ask you one or two plain questions, to which I beg that you will give a plain answer.'

'Certainly, madam.'

'Do not trouble about my feelings. I am not hysterical, nor given to fainting. I simply wish to hear your real, real opinion.'

'Upon what point?'

'In your heart of hearts, do you think that Neville is alive?'

Sherlock Holmes seemed to be embarrassed by the question. 'Frankly, now!' she repeated, standing upon the rug and looking keenly down at him as he leaned back in a basket-chair.

'Frankly, then, madam, I do not.'

'You think that he is dead?'

'I do.'

'Murdered?'

'I don't say that. Perhaps.'

'And on what day did he meet his death?'

'On Monday.'

'Then perhaps, Mr Holmes, you will be good enough to explain how it is that I have received a letter from him today.'

Sherlock Holmes sprang out of his chair as if he had been galvanized.

'What!' he roared.

'Yes, today.' She stood smiling, holding up a little slip of paper in the air.

'May I see it?'

'Certainly.'

He snatched it from her in his eagerness, and smoothing it out upon the table he drew over the lamp and examined it intently. I had left my chair and was gazing at it over his shoulder.

The envelope was a very coarse one and was stamped with the Gravesend postmark and with the date of that very day, or rather of the day before, for it was considerably after midnight.

'Coarse writing,' murmured Holmes. 'Surely this is not your husband's writing, madam.'

'No, but the enclosure is.'

'I perceive also that whoever addressed the envelope had to go and inquire as to the address.'

'How can you tell that?'

'The name, you see, is in perfectly black ink, which has dried itself. The rest is of the grayish colour, which shows that blotting-paper has been used. If it had been written straight off, and then blotted, none would be of a deep black shade. This man has written the name, and there has then been a pause before he wrote the address, which can only mean that he was not familiar with it. It is, of course, a trifle, but there is nothing so important as trifles. Let us now see the letter. Ha! There has been an enclosure here!'

'Yes, there was a ring. His signet-ring.'

'And you are sure that this is your husband's hand?'

'One of his hands.'

'One?'

'His hand when he wrote hurriedly. It is very unlike his usual writing, and yet I know it well.'

Dearest do not be frightened. All will come well. There is a huge error which it may take some little time to rectify. Wait in patience. NEVILLE.

Written in pencil upon the fly-leaf of a book, octavo size, no water-mark. Hum! Posted today in Gravesend by a man with a dirty thumb. Ha! And the flap has been gummed, if I am not very much in error, by a person who had been chewing tobacco. And you have no doubt that it is your husband's hand, madam?'

'None. Neville wrote those words.'

'And they were posted today at Gravesend. Well, Mrs St. Clair, the clouds lighten, though I should not venture to say that the danger is over.'

'But he must be alive, Mr Holmes.'

'Unless this is a clever forgery to put us on the wrong scent. The ring, after all, proves nothing. It may have been taken from him.

'No, no; it is, it is his very own writing!'

'Very well. It may, however, have been written on Monday and only posted today.'

'That is possible.'

'If so, much may have happened between.'

'Oh, you must not discourage me, Mr Holmes. I know that all is well with him. There is so keen a sympathy between us that I should know if evil came upon him. On the very day that I saw him last he cut himself in the bedroom, and yet I in the dining room rushed upstairs instantly with the utmost certainty that something had happened. Do you think that I would respond to such a trifle and yet be ignorant of his death?'

'I have seen too much not to know that the impression of a woman may be more valuable than the conclusion of an analytical reasoner. And in this letter you certainly have a very strong piece of evidence to corroborate your view. But if your husband is alive and able to write letters, why should he remain away from you?'

'I cannot imagine. It is unthinkable.'

'And on Monday he made no remarks before leaving you?'

'No.'

'And you were surprised to see him in Swandam Lane?'

'Very much so.'

'Was the window open?'

'Yes.'

'Then he might have called to you?'

'He might.'

'He only, as I understand, gave an inarticulate cry?'

'Yes.'

'A call for help, you thought?'

'Yes. He waved his hands.'

'But it might have been a cry of surprise. Astonishment at the unexpected sight of you might cause him to throw up his hands?'

'It is possible.'

'And you thought he was pulled back?'

'He disappeared so suddenly.'

'He might have leaped back. You did not see anyone else in the room?'

'No, but this horrible man confessed to having been there, and the lascar was at the foot of the stairs.'

'Quite so. Your husband, as far as you could see, had his ordinary clothes on?'

'But without his collar or tie. I distinctly saw his bare throat.'

'Had he ever spoken of Swandam Lane?'

'Never.'

'Had he ever showed any signs of having taken opium?'

'Never.'

'Thank you, Mrs St. Clair. Those are the principal points about which I wished to be absolutely clear. We shall now have a little supper and then retire, for we may have a very busy day tomorrow.'

A large and comfortable double-bedded room had been placed at our disposal, and I was quickly between the sheets, for I was weary after my night of adventure. Sherlock Holmes was a man, however, who, when he had an unsolved problem upon his mind, would go for days, and even for a week, without rest, turning it over, rearranging his facts, looking at it from every point of view until he had either fathomed it or convinced himself that his data were insufficient. It was soon evident to me that he was now preparing for an all-night sitting. He took off his coat and waistcoat, put on a large blue dressing-gown, and then wandered about the room collecting pillows from his bed and cushions from the sofa and armchairs. With these he constructed a sort of Eastern divan, upon which he perched himself cross-legged, with an ounce of shag tobacco and a box of matches laid out in front of him. In the dim light of the lamp I saw him sitting there, an old briar pipe between his lips, his eyes fixed vacantly upon the corner of the ceiling, the blue smoke curling up from him, silent, motionless, with the light shining upon his strong-set aquiline features. So he sat as I dropped off to sleep, and so he sat when a sudden ejaculation caused me to wake up, and I found the summer sun shining into the apartment. The pipe was still between his lips, the smoke still curled upward, and the room was full of a dense tobacco haze, but nothing remained of the heap of shag which I had seen upon the previous night.

'Awake, Watson?' he asked.

'Yes.'

'Game for a morning drive?'

'Certainly.'

'Then dress. No one is stirring yet, but I know where the stable-boy sleeps, and we shall soon have the trap out.' He chuckled to himself as he spoke, his eyes twinkled, and he seemed a different man to the sombre thinker of the previous night.

As I dressed I glanced at my watch. It was no wonder that no one was stirring. It was twenty-five minutes past four. I had hardly finished when Holmes returned with the news that the boy was putting in the horse.

'I want to test a little theory of mine,' said he, pulling on his boots. 'I think, Watson, that you are now standing in the presence of one of the most absolute fools in Europe. I deserve to be kicked from here to Charing Cross. But I think I have the key of the affair now.'

'And where is it?' I asked, smiling.

'In the bathroom,' he answered. 'Oh, yes, I am not joking,' he continued, seeing my look of incredulity. 'I have just been there, and I have taken it out, and I have got it in this Gladstone bag. Come on, my boy, and we shall see whether it will not fit the lock.'

We made our way downstairs as quietly as possible, and out into the bright morning sunshine. In the road stood our horse and trap, with the half-clad stable boy waiting at the head. We both sprang in, and away we dashed down the London Road. A few country carts were stirring, bearing in vegetables to the metropolis, but the lines of villas on either side were as silent and lifeless as some city in a dream.

'It has been in some points a singular case,' said Holmes, flicking the horse on into a gallop. 'I confess that I have been as blind as a mole, but it is better to learn wisdom late than never to learn it at all.'

In town the earliest risers were just beginning to look sleepily from their windows as we drove through the streets of the Surrey side. Passing down the Waterloo Bridge Road we crossed over the river, and dashing up Wellington Street wheeled sharply to the right and found ourselves in Bow Street. Sherlock Holmes was well known to the force, and the two constables at the door saluted him. One of them held the horse's head while the other led us in.

'Who is on duty?' asked Holmes.

'Inspector Bradstreet, sir.'

'Ah, Bradstreet, how are you?' A tall, stout official had come down the stone-flagged passage, in a peaked cap and frogged jacket. 'I wish to have a quiet word with you, Bradstreet.' 'Certainly, Mr Holmes. Step into my room here.' It was a small, office-like room, with a huge ledger upon the table, and a telephone projecting from the wall. The inspector sat down at his desk.

'What can I do for you, Mr Holmes?'

'I called about that beggarman, Boone—the one who was

charged with being concerned in the disappearance of Mr Neville St. Clair, of Lee.'

'Yes. He was brought up and remanded for further inquiries.'

'So I heard. You have him here?'

'In the cells.'

'Is he quiet?'

'Oh, he gives no trouble. But he is a dirty scoundrel.'

'Dirty?'

'Yes, it is all we can do to make him wash his hands, and his face is as black as a tinker's. Well, when once his case has been settled, he will have a regular prison bath; and I think, if you saw him, you would agree with me that he needed it.'

'I should like to see him very much.'

'Would you? That is easily done. Come this way. You can leave your bag.'

'No, I think that I'll take it.'

'Very good. Come this way, if you please.' He led us down a passage, opened a barred door, passed down a winding stair, and brought us to a whitewashed corridor with a line of doors on each side.

'The third on the right is his,' said the inspector. 'Here it is!' He quietly shot back a panel in the upper part of the door and glanced through.

'He is asleep,' said he. 'You can see him very well.'

We both put our eyes to the grating. The prisoner lay with his face towards us, in a very deep sleep, breathing slowly and heavily. He was a middle-sized man, coarsely clad as became his calling, with a coloured shirt protruding through the rent in his tattered coat. He was, as the inspector had said, extremely dirty, but the grime which covered his face could not conceal its repulsive ugliness. A broad wheal from an old scar ran right across it from eye to chin, and by its contraction had turned up one side of the upper lip, so that three teeth were exposed in a perpetual snarl. A shock of very bright red hair grew low over his eyes and forehead.

'He's a beauty, isn't he?' said the inspector.

'He certainly needs a wash,' remarked Holmes. 'I had an idea that he might, and I took the liberty of bringing the tools with me.' He opened the Gladstone bag as he spoke, and took out, to my astonishment, a very large bath-sponge.

'He! he! You are a funny one,' chuckled the inspector.

'Now, if you will have the great goodness to open that door very quietly, we will soon make him cut a much more respectable figure.'

'Well, I don't know why not,' said the inspector. 'He doesn't look a credit to the Bow Street cells, does he?' He slipped his key into the lock, and we all very quietly entered the cell. The sleeper half turned, and then settled down once more into a deep slumber. Holmes stooped to the waterjug, moistened his sponge, and then rubbed it twice vigorously across and down the prisoner's face.

'Let me introduce you,' he shouted, 'to Mr Neville St. Clair, of Lee, in the county of Kent.'

Never in my life have I seen such a sight. The man's face peeled off under the sponge like the bark from a tree. Gone was the coarse brown tint! Gone, too, was the horrid scar which had seamed it across, and the twisted lip which had given the repulsive sneer to the face! A twitch brought away the tangled red hair, and there, sitting up in his bed, was a pale, sad-faced, refined-looking man, black-haired and smooth-skinned, rubbing his eyes and staring about him with sleepy bewilderment. Then suddenly realizing the exposure, he broke into a scream and threw himself down with his face to the pillow.

'Great heavens!' cried the inspector, 'it is, indeed, the missing man. I know him from the photograph.'

The prisoner turned with the reckless air of a man who abandons himself to his destiny. 'Be it so,' said he. 'And pray what am I charged with?'

'With making away with Mr Neville St.—Oh, come, you can't be charged with that unless they make a case of attempted suicide of it,' said the inspector with a grin. 'Well, I have been twenty-seven years in the force, but this really takes the cake.'

'If I am Mr Neville St. Clair, then it is obvious that no crime has been committed, and that, therefore, I am illegally detained.'

'No crime, but a very great error has been committed,' said Holmes. 'You would have done better to have trusted your wife.'

'It was not the wife; it was the children,' groaned the prisoner. 'God help me, I would not have them ashamed of their father. My God! What an exposure! What can I do?'

Sherlock Holmes sat down beside him on the couch and patted him kindly on the shoulder.

'If you leave it to a court of law to clear the matter up,' said he, 'of course you can hardly avoid publicity. On the other hand, if you convince the police authorities that there is no possible case against you, I do not know that there is any reason that the details should find their way into the papers. Inspector Bradstreet would, I am sure, make notes upon anything which you might tell us and submit it to the proper authorities. The case would then never go into court at all.'

'God bless you!' cried the prisoner passionately. 'I would have endured imprisonment, ay, even execution, rather than have left my miserable secret as a family blot to my children.

'You are the first who have ever heard my story. My father was a school-master in Chesterfield, where I received an excellent education. I travelled in my youth, took to the stage, and finally became a reporter on an evening paper in London. One day my editor wished to have a series of articles upon begging in the metropolis, and I volunteered to supply them. There was the point from which all my adventures started. It was only by trying begging as an amateur that I could get the facts upon which to base my articles. When an actor I had, of course, learned all the secrets of making up, and had been famous in the green-room for my skill. I took advantage now of my attainments. I painted my face, and to make myself as pitiable as possible, I made a good scar and fixed one side of my lip in a twist by the aid of a small slip of flesh-coloured plaster. Then with a red head of hair, and an appropriate dress, I took my station in the business part of the city, ostensibly as a match-seller but really as a beggar. For seven hours I plied my trade, and when I returned home in the evening, I found to my surprise that I had received no less than 26s. 4d.

'I wrote my articles and thought little more of the matter until, some time later, I backed a bill for a friend and had a writ served upon me for £25. I was at my wit's end where to get the money, but a sudden idea came to me. I begged a fortnight's grace from the creditor, asked for a holiday from my employers, and spent the time in begging in the City under my disguise. In ten days I had the money and had paid the debt.

'Well, you can imagine how hard it was to settle down to arduous work at £2 a week when I knew that I could earn as much in a day by smearing my face with a little paint, laying my cap on the ground, and sitting still. It was a long fight between my pride and the money, but the dollars won at last, and I threw up reporting and sat day after day in the corner which I had first chosen, inspiring pity by my ghastly face and filling my pockets with coppers. Only one man knew my secret. He was the keeper of a low den in which I used to lodge in Swandam Lane, where I could every morning emerge as a squalid beggar and in the evenings transform myself into a well-dressed man about town. This fellow, a lascar, was well paid by me for his rooms, so that I knew that my secret was safe in his possession.

'Well, very soon I found that I was saving considerable sums of money. I do not mean that any beggar in the streets of London could earn 700 pounds a year—which is less than my average takings—but I had exceptional advantages in my power of making up, and also in a facility of repartee, which improved by practice and made me quite a recognized character in the City. All day a stream of pennies, varied by silver, poured in upon me, and it was a very bad day in which I failed to take £2.

'As I grew richer I grew more ambitious, took a house in the country, and eventually married, without anyone having a suspicion as to my real occupation. My dear wife knew that I had business in the City. She little knew what.

'Last Monday I had finished for the day and was dressing in my room above the opium den when I looked out of my window and saw, to my horror and astonishment, that my wife was standing in the street, with her eyes fixed full upon me. I gave a cry of surprise, threw up my arms to cover my face, and, rushing to my confidant, the lascar, entreated him to prevent anyone from coming up to me. I heard her voice downstairs, but I knew that she could not ascend. Swiftly, I threw off my clothes, pulled on those of a beggar, and put on my pigments and wig. Even a wife's eyes could not pierce so complete a disguise. But then it occurred to me that there might be a search in the room, and that the clothes might betray me. I threw open the window, reopening by my violence a small cut which I had inflicted upon myself in the bedroom that morning. Then I seized my coat, which was weighted by the coppers which I had just transferred to it from the leather bag in which I carried my takings. I hurled it out of the window, and it disappered into the Thames. The other clothes would have followed, but at that moment there was a rush of constables up the stairs, and a few minutes after I found, rather, I confess, to my relief, that instead of being identified as Mr Neville St. Clair, I was arrested as his murderer.

'I do not know that there is anything else for me to explain. I was determined to preserve my disguise as long as possible, and hence my preference for a dirty face. Knowing that my wife would be terribly anxious, I slipped off my ring and confided it to the lascar at a moment when no constable was watching me, together with a hurried scrawl, telling her that she had no cause to fear.'

'That note only reached her yesterday,' said Holmes.

'Good God! What a week she must have spent!'

'The police have watched this lascar,' said Inspector Bradstreet, 'and I can quite understand that he might find it difficult to post a letter unobserved. Probably he handed it to some sailor customer of his, who forgot all about it for some days.'

'That was it,' said Holmes, nodding approvingly; 'I have no doubt of it. But have you never been prosecuted for begging?'

'Many times; but what was a fine to me?'

'It must stop here, however,' said Bradstreet. 'If the police are to hush this thing up, there must be no more of Hugh Boone.'

'I have sworn it by the most solemn oaths which a man can take.'

'In that case I think that it is probable that no further steps may be taken. But if you are found again, then all must come out. I am sure, Mr Holmes, that we are very much indebted to you for having cleared the matter up. I wish I knew how you reach your results.'

'I reached this one,' said my friend, 'by sitting upon five pillows and consuming an ounce of shag. I think, Watson, that if we drive to Baker Street we shall just be in time for breakfast.'

A CASE OF IDENTITY

'My dear fellow.' said Sherlock Holmes as we sat on either side of the fire in his lodgings at Baker Street, 'life is infinitely stranger than anything which the mind of man could invent. We would not dare to conceive the things which are really mere commonplaces of existence. If we could fly out of that window hand in hand, hover over this great city, gently remove the roofs, and peep in at the queer things which are going on, the strange coincidences, the plannings, the cross-purposes, the wonderful chains of events, working through generation, and leading to the most outre results, it would make all fiction with its conventionalities and foreseen conclusions most stale and unprofitable.'

'And yet I am not convinced of it,' I answered. 'The cases which come to light in the papers are, as a rule, bald enough, and vulgar enough. We have in our police reports realism pushed to its extreme limits, and yet the result is, it must be confessed, neither fascinating nor artistic.'

'A certain selection and discretion must be used in producing a realistic effect,' remarked Holmes. 'This is wanting in the police report, where more stress is laid, perhaps, upon the platitudes of the magistrate than upon the details, which to an observer contain the vital essence of the whole matter. Depend upon it, there is nothing so unnatural as the commonplace.'

I smiled and shook my head. 'I can quite understand your thinking so.' I said. 'Of course, in your position of unofficial adviser and helper to everybody who is absolutely puzzled, throughout three continents, you are brought in contact with all that is strange and bizarre. But here'—I picked up the morning paper from the ground—'let us put it to a practical test. Here is the first heading upon which I come. "A husband's cruelty to his wife." There is half a column of print, but I know without reading it that it is all perfectly familiar to me. There is. Of course, the other woman, the drink, the push, the blow, the bruise, the sympathetic sister or landlady. The crudest of writers could invent nothing more crude.'

'Indeed, your example is an unfortunate one for your argument,' said Holmes, taking the paper and glancing his eye down it. 'This is the Dundas separation case, and, as it happens, I was engaged in clearing up some small points in connection with it. The husband was a teetotaler, there was no other woman, and the conduct complained of was that he had drifted into the habit of winding up every meal by taking out his false teeth and hurling them at his wife, which, you will allow, is not an action likely to occur to the imagination of the average story-teller. Take a pinch of snuff, Doctor, and acknowledge that I have scored over you in your example.'

He held out his snuffbox of old gold, with a great amethyst in the centre of the lid. Its splendour was in such contrast to his homely ways and simple life that I could not help commenting upon it.

'Ah,' said he, 'I forgot that I had not seen you for some weeks. It is a little souvenir from the King of Bohemia in return for my assistance in the case of the Irene Adler papers.'

'And the ring?' I asked, glancing at a remarkable brilliant which sparkled upon his finger.

'It was from the reigning family of Holland, though the matter in which I served them was of such delicacy that I cannot confide it even to you, who have been good enough to chronicle one or two of my little problems.'

'And have you any on hand just now?' I asked with interest.

'Some ten or twelve, but none which present any feature of interest. They are important, you understand, without being interesting. Indeed, I have found that it is usually in unimportant matters that there is a field for the observation, and for the quick analysis of cause and effect which gives the charm to an investigation. The larger crimes are apt to be the simpler, for the bigger the crime the more obvious, as a rule, is the motive. In these cases, save for one rather intricate matter which has been referred to me from Marseilles, there is nothing which presents any features of interest. It is possible, however, that I may have something better before very many minutes are over, for this is one of my clients, or I am much mistaken.'

He had risen from his chair and was standing between the parted blinds gazing down into the dull neutral-tinted London street. Looking over his shoulder, I saw that on the pavement opposite there stood a large woman with a heavy fur boa round her neck, and a large curling red feather in a broad-brimmed hat which was tilted in a coquettish Duchess of Devonshire fashion over her ear. From under this great panoply she peeped up in a nervous, hesitating fashion at our windows, while her body oscillated backward and forward, and her fingers fidgeted with her glove buttons. Suddenly, with a plunge, as of the swimmer who leaves the bank, she hurried across the road, and we heard the sharp clang of the bell.

'I have seen those symptoms before,' said Holmes, throwing his cigarette into the fire. 'Oscillation upon the pavement always means an affaire de coeur. She would like advice, but is not sure that the matter is not too delicate for communication. And yet even here we may discriminate. When a woman has been seriously wronged by a man she no longer oscillates, and the usual symptom is a broken bell wire. Here we may take it that there is a love matter, but that the maiden is not so much angry as perplexed, or grieved. But here she comes in person to resolve our doubts.'

As he spoke there was a tap at the door, and the boy in buttons. entered to announce Miss Mary Sutherland, while the lady herself loomed behind his small black figure like a full-sailed merchantman behind a tiny pilot boat. Sherlock Holmes welcomed her with the easy courtesy for which he was remarkable, and, having closed the door and bowed her into an armchair, he looked her over in the minute and yet abstracted fashion which was peculiar to him.

'Do you not find,' he said, 'that with your short sight it is a little trying to do so much typewriting?'

'I did at first,' she answered, 'but now I know where the letters are without looking.' Then, suddenly realizing the full purport of his words, she gave a violent start and looked up, with fear and astonishment upon her broad, good-humoured face. 'You've heard about me, Mr Holmes,' she cried, 'else how could you know all that?'

'Never mind,' said Holmes, laughing; 'it is my business to know things. Perhaps I have trained myself to see what others overlook. If not, why should you come to consult me?'

'I came to you, sir, because I heard of you from Mrs Etherege, whose husband you found so easy when the police and everyone had given him up for dead. Oh, Mr Holmes, I wish you would do as much for me. I'm not rich, but still I have a hundred a year in my own right, besides the little that I make by the machine, and I would give it all to know what has become of Mr Hosmer Angel.'

'Why did you come away to consult me in such a hurry?' asked Sherlock Holmes, with his finger-tips together and his eyes to the ceiling.

Again a startled look came over the somewhat vacuous face of Miss Mary Sutherland. 'Yes, I did bang out of the house,' she said, 'for it made me angry to see the easy way in which Mr Windibank—that is, my father—took it all. He would not go to the police, and he would not go to you, and so at last, as he would do nothing and kept on saying that there was no harm done, it made me mad, and I just on with my things and came right away to you.'

'Your father,' said Holmes, 'your stepfather, surely, since the name is different.'

'Yes, my stepfather. I call him father, though it sounds funny, too, for he is only five years and two months older than myself. '

'And your mother is alive?'

'Oh, yes, mother is alive and well. I wasn't best pleased, Mr Holmes, when she married again so soon after father's death, and a man who was nearly fifteen years younger than herself. Father was a plumber in the Tottenham Court Road, and he left a tidy business behind him, which mother carried on with Mr Hardy, the foreman; but when Mr Windibank came he made her sell the business, for he was very superior, being a traveller in wines. They got £4700 for the goodwill and interest, which wasn't near as much as father could have got if he had been alive.'

I had expected to see Sherlock Holmes impatient under this rambling and inconsequential narrative, but, on the contrary he had listened with the greatest concentration of attention.

'Your own little income,' he asked, 'does it come out of the business?'

'Oh, no, sir. It is quite separate and was left me by my Uncle Ned in Auckland. It is in New Zealand stock, paying 4 1/2 per cent. Two thousand five hundred pounds was the amount, but I can only touch the interest.'

'You interest me extremely,' said Holmes. 'And since you draw so large a sum as a hundred a year, with what you earn into the bargain, you no doubt travel a little and indulge yourself in every way. I believe that a single lady can get on very nicely upon an income of about £60.'

'I could do with much less than that, Mr Holmes, but you understand that as long as I live at home I don't wish to be a burden to them, and so they have the use of the money just while I am staying with them. Of course, that is only just for the time. Mr Windibank draws my interest every quarter and pays it over to mother, and I find that I can do pretty well with what I earn at typewriting. It brings me twopence a sheet, and I can often do from fifteen to twenty sheets in a day.'

'You have made your position very clear to me,' said Holmes. 'This is my friend, Dr. Watson, before whom you can speak as freely as before myself. Kindly tell us now all about your connection with Mr Hosmer Angel.'

A flush stole over Miss Sutherland's face, and she picked nervously at the fringe of her jacket. 'I met him first at the gasfitters' ball,' she said. 'They used to send father tickets when he was alive, and then afterwards they remembered us, and sent them to mother. Mr Windibank did not wish us to go. He never did wish us to go anywhere. He would get quite mad if I wanted so much as to join a Sunday school treat. But this time I was set on going, and I would go; for what right had he to prevent? He said the folk were not fit for us to know, when all father's friends were to be there. And he said that I had nothing fit to wear, when I had my purple plush that I had never so much as taken out of the drawer. At last, when nothing else would do, he went off to France upon the business of the firm, but we went, mother and I, with Mr Hardy, who used to be our foreman, and it was there I met Mr Hosmer Angel.'

'I suppose,' said Holmes, 'that when Mr Windibank came back from France he was very annoyed at your having gone to the ball.'

'Oh, well, he was very good about it. He laughed, I remember, and shrugged his shoulders, and said there was no use denying anything to a woman, for she would have her way.'

'I see. Then at the gasfitters' ball you met, as I understand, a gentleman called Mr Hosmer Angel.'

'Yes, sir. I met him that night, and he called next day to ask if we had got home all safe, and after that we met him—that is to say, Mr Holmes, I met him twice for walks, but after that father came back again, and Mr Hosmer Angel could not come to the house any more.'

'No?'

'Well, you know father didn't like anything of the sort. He wouldn't have any visitors if he could help it, and he used to say that a woman should be happy in her own family circle. But then, as I used to say to mother, a woman wants her own circle to begin with, and I had not got mine yet.'

'But how about Mr Hosmer Angel? Did he make no attempt to see you?'

'Well, father was going off to France again in a week, and Hosmer wrote and said that it would be safer and better not to see each other until he had gone. We could write in the meantime, and he used to write every day. I took the letters in in the morning, so there was no need for father to know.'

'Were you engaged to the gentleman at this time?'

'Oh, yes, Mr Holmes. We were engaged after the first walk that we took. Hosmer—Mr Angel—was a cashier in an office in Leadenhall Street—and—'

'What office?'

'That's the worst of it, Mr Holmes, I don't know.'

'Where did he live, then?'

'He slept on the premises.'

'And you don't know his address?'

'No—except that it was Leadenhall Street.'

'Where did you address your letters, then?'

'To the Leadenhall Street Post-Office, to be left till called for. He said that if they were sent to the office he would be chaffed by all the other clerks about having letters from a lady, so I offered to typewrite them, like he did his, but he wouldn't have that, for he said that when I wrote them they seemed to come from me, but when they were typewritten he always felt that the machine had come between us. That will just show you how fond he was of me, Mr Holmes, and the little things that he would think of.'

'It was most suggestive,' said Holmes. 'It has long been an axiom of mine that the little things are infinitely the most important. Can you remember any other little things about Mr Hosmer Angel?'

'He was a very shy man, Mr Holmes. He would rather walk with me in the evening than in the daylight, for he said that he hated to be conspicuous. Very retiring and gentlemanly he was. Even his voice was gentle. He'd had the quinsy and swollen glands when he was young, he told me, and it had left him with a weak throat, and a hesitating, whispering fashion of speech. He was always well dressed, very neat and plain, but his eyes were weak, just as mine are, and he wore tinted glasses against the glare.'

'Well, and what happened when Mr Windibank, your stepfather, returned to France?'

'Mr Hosmer Angel came to the house again and proposed that we should marry before father came back. He was in dreadful earnest and made me swear, with my hands on the Testament, that whatever happened I would always be true to him. Mother said he was quite right to make me swear, and that it was a sign of his passion. Mother was all in his favour from the first and was even fonder of him than I was. Then, when they talked of marrying within the week, I began to ask about father; but they both said never to mind about father, but just to tell him afterwards, and mother said she would make it all right with him. I didn't quite like that, Mr Holmes. It seemed funny that I should ask his leave, as he was only a few years older than me; but I didn't want to do anything on the sly, so l wrote to father at Bordeaux, where the company has its French offices, but the letter came back to me on the very morning of the wedding.'

'It missed him, then?'

'Yes, sir; for he had started to England just before it arrived.'

'Ha! That was unfortunate. Your wedding was arranged, then, for the Friday. Was it to be in church?'

'Yes, sir, but very quietly. It was to be at St. Saviour's, near King's Cross, and we were to have breakfast afterwards at the St. Pancras Hotel. Hosmer came for us in a hansom, but as there were two of us he put us both into it and stepped himself into a four-wheeler, which happened to be the only other cab in the street. We got to the church first, and when the four-wheeler drove up we waited for him to step out, but he never did, and when the cabman got down from the box and looked there was no one there! The cabman said that he could not imagine what had become of him, for he had seen him get in with his own eyes. That was last Friday, Mr Holmes, and I have never seen or heard anything since then to throw any light upon what became of him.'

'It seems to me that you have been very shamefully treated,' said Holmes.

'Oh, no, sir! He was too good and kind to leave me so. Why, all the morning he was saying to me that, whatever happened, I was to be true; and that even if something quite unforeseen occurred to separate us, I was always to remember that I was pledged to him, and that he would claim his pledge sooner or later. It seemed strange talk for a wedding-morning, but what has happened since gives a meaning to it.'

'Most certainly it does. Your own opinion is, then, that some unforeseen catastrophe has occurred to him?'

'Yes, sir. I believe that he foresaw some danger, or else he would not have talked so. And then I think that what he foresaw happened.'

'But you have no notion as to what it could have been?'

'None.'

'One more question. How did your mother take the matter?'

'She was angry, and said that I was never to speak of the matter again.'

'And your father? Did you tell him?'

'Yes; and he seemed to think, with me, that something had happened, and that I should hear of Hosmer again. As he said, what interest could anyone have in bringing me to the doors of the church, and then leaving me? Now, if he had borrowed my money, or if he had married me and got my money settled on him, there might be some reason, but Hosmer was very independent about money and never would look at a shilling of mine. And yet, what could have happened? And why could he not write? Oh, it drives me half-mad to think of it, and I can't sleep a wink at night.' She pulled a little handkerchief out of her muff and began to sob heavily into it.

'I shall glance into the case for you,' said Holmes, rising, 'and I have no doubt that we shall reach some definite result. Let the weight of the matter rest upon me now, and do not let your mind dwell upon it further. Above all, try to let Mr Hosmer Angel vanish from your memory, as he has done from your life.'

'Then you don't think I'll see him again?'

'I fear not.'

'Then what has happened to him?'

'You will leave that question in my hands. I should like an accurate description of him and any letters of his which you can spare.'

'I advertised for him in last Saturday's *Chronicle*,' said she. 'Here is the slip and here are four letters from him.'

'Thank you. And your address?'

'No. 31 Lyon Place, Camberwell.'

'Mr Angel's address you never had, I understand. Where is your father's place of business?'

'He travels for Westhouse & Marbank, the great claret

importers of Fenchurch Street.'

'Thank you. You have made your statement very clearly. You will leave the papers here, and remember the advice which I have given you. Let the whole incident be a sealed book, and do not allow it to affect your life.'

'You are very kind, Mr Holmes, but I cannot do that. I shall be true to Hosmer. He shall find me ready when he comes back.'

For all the preposterous hat and the vacuous face, there was something noble in the simple faith of our visitor which compelled our respect. She laid her little bundle of papers upon the table and went her way, with a promise to come again whenever she might be summoned.

Sherlock Holmes sat silent for a few minutes with his fingertips still pressed together, his legs stretched out in front of him, and his gaze directed upward to the ceiling. Then he took down from the rack the old and oily clay pipe, which was to him as a counsellor, and, having lit it, he leaned back in his chair, with the thick blue cloud-wreaths spinning up from him, and a look of infinite languor in his face.

'Quite an interesting study, that maiden,' he observed. 'I found her more interesting than her little problem, which, by the way, is rather a trite one. You will find parallel cases, if you consult my index, in Andover in '77, and there was something of the sort at The Hague last year. Old as is the idea, however, there were one or two details which were new to me. But the maiden herself was most instructive.'

'You appeared to read a good deal upon her which was quite invisible to me,' I remarked.

'Not invisible but unnoticed, Watson. You did not know where to look, and so you missed all that was important. I can never bring you to realize the importance of sleeves, the suggestiveness of thumb-nails, or the great issues that may hang from a boot-lace. Now, what did you gather from that woman's appearance?

Describe it.'

'Well, she had a slate-coloured, broad-brimmed straw hat, with a feather of a brickish red. Her jacket was black, with black beads sewn upon it, and a fringe of little black jet ornaments. Her dress was brown, rather darker than coffee colour, with a little purple plush at the neck and sleeves. Her gloves were grayish and were worn through at the right forefinger. Her boots I didn't observe. She had small round, hanging gold earrings, and a general air of being fairly well-to-do in a vulgar, comfortable, easy-going way.'

Sherlock Holmes clapped his hands softly together and chuckled.

'"Pon my word, Watson, you are coming along wonderfully. You have really done very well indeed. It is true that you have missed everything of importance, but you have hit upon the method, and you have a quick eye for colour. Never trust to general impressions, my boy, but concentrate yourself upon details. My first glance is always at a woman's sleeve. In a man it is perhaps better first to take the knee of the trouser. As you observe, this woman had plush upon her sleeves, which is a most useful material for showing traces. The double line a little above the wrist, where the typewritist presses against the table, was beautifully defined. The sewing-machine, of the hand type, leaves a similar mark, but only on the left arm, and on the side of it farthest from the thumb, instead of being right across the broadest part, as this was. I then glanced at her face, and, observing the dint of a pince-nez at either side of her nose, I ventured a remark upon short sight and typewriting, which seemed to surprise her.'

'It surprised me.'

'But, surely, it was obvious. I was then much surprised and interested on glancing down to observe that, though the boots which she was wearing were not unlike each other, they were really odd ones; the one having a slightly decorated toe-cap, and the other a plain one. One was buttoned only in the two lower buttons out of five, and the other at the first, third, and fifth. Now, when you see that a young lady, otherwise neatly dressed, has come away from home with odd boots, half-buttoned, it is no great deduction to say that she came away in a hurry.'

'And what else?' I asked, keenly interested, as I always was, by my friend's incisive reasoning.

'I noted, in passing, that she had written a note before leaving home but after being fully dressed. You observed that her right glove was torn at the forefinger, but you did not apparently see that both glove and finger were stained with violet ink. She had written in a hurry and dipped her pen too deep. It must have been this morning, or the mark would not remain clear upon the finger. All this is amusing, though rather elementary, but I must go back to business, Watson. Would you mind reading me the advertised description of Mr Hosmer Angel?'

I held the little printed slip to the light.

'"Missing", it said on the morning of the fourteenth, a gentleman named Hosmer Angel. About five feet seven inches in height; strongly built, sallow complexion, black hair, a little bald in the centre, bushy, black side-whiskers and moustache; tinted glasses, slight infirmity of speech. Was dressed, when last seen, in black frock-coat faced with silk, black waistcoat, gold Albert chain, and gray Harris tweed trousers, with brown gaiters over elastic-sided boots. Known to have been employed in an office in Leadenhall Street. Anybody bringing—' 'That will do,' said Holmes. 'As to the letters,' he continued, glancing over them, 'they are very commonplace. Absolutely no clue in them to Mr Angel, save that he quotes Balzac once. There is one remarkable point, however, which will no doubt strike you.'

'They are typewritten,' I remarked.

'Not only that, but the signature is typewritten. Look at the neat little "Hosmer Angel" at the bottom. There is a date, you see, but no superscription except Leadenhall Street, which is rather vague. The point about the signature is very suggestive—in fact, we may call it conclusive.'

'Of what?'

'My dear fellow, is it possible you do not see how strongly it bears upon the case?'

'I cannot say that I do unless it were that he wished to be able to deny his signature if an action for breach of promise were instituted.'

'No, that was not the point. However, I shall write two letters, which should settle the matter. One is to a firm in the City, the other is to the young lady's stepfather, Mr Windibank, asking him whether he could meet us here at six o'clock tomorrow evening. It is just as well that we should do business with the male relatives. And now, Doctor, we can do nothing until the answers to those letters come, so we may put our little problem upon the shelf for the interim.'

I had had so many reasons to believe in my friend's subtle powers of reasoning and extraordinary energy in action that I felt that he must have some solid grounds for the assured and easy demeanour with which he treated the singular mystery which he had been called upon to fathom. Once only had I known him to fail, in the case of the King of Bohemia and of the Irene Adler photograph; but when I looked back to the weird business of "The Sign of Four", and the extraordinary circumstances connected with "A Study in Scarlet", I felt that it would be a strange tangle indeed which he could not unravel.

I left him then, still puffing at his black clay pipe, with the conviction that when I came again on the next evening I would find that he held in his hands all the clues which would lead up to the identity of the disappearing bridegroom of Miss Mary Sutherland.

A professional case of great gravity was engaging my own attention at the time, and the whole of next day I was busy at the bedside of the sufferer. It was not until close upon six o'clock that I found myself free and was able to spring into a hansom and drive to Baker Street, half afraid that I might be too late to assist at the denouement of the little mystery. I found Sherlock Holmes alone, however, half asleep, with his long, thin form curled up in the recesses of his armchair. A formidable array of bottles and test-tubes, with the pungent cleanly smell of hydrochloric acid, told me that he had spent his day in the chemical work which was so dear to him.

'Well, have you solved it?' I asked as I entered.

'Yes. It was the bisulphate of baryta.'

'No, no, the mystery!' I cried.

'Oh, that! I thought of the salt that I have been working upon. There was never any mystery in the matter, though, as I said yesterday, some of the details are of interest. The only drawback is that there is no law, I fear, that can touch the scoundrel.'

'Who was he, then, and what was his object in deserting Miss Sutherland?'

The question was hardly out of my mouth, and Holmes had not yet opened his lips to reply, when we heard a heavy footfall in the passage and a tap at the door.

'This is the girl's stepfather, Mr James Windibank,' said Holmes. 'He has written to me to say that he would be here at six. Come in!'

The man who entered was a sturdy, middle-sized fellow, some thirty years of age, clean-shaven, and sallow-skinned, with a bland, insinuating manner, and a pair of wonderfully sharp and penetrating gray eyes. He shot a questioning glance at each of us, placed his shiny top-hat upon the sideboard, and with a slight bow sidled down into the nearest chair.

'Good-evening, Mr James Windibank,' said Holmes. 'I think that this typewritten letter is from you, in which you made an appointment with me for six o'clock?'

'Yes, sir. I am afraid that I am a little late, but I am not quite my own master, you know. I am sorry that Miss Sutherland has troubled you about this little matter, for I think it is far better not to wash linen of the sort in public. It was quite against my wishes that she came, but she is a very excitable, impulsive girl, as you may have noticed, and she is not easily controlled when she has made up her mind on a point. Of course, I did not mind you so much, as you are not connected with the official police, but it is not pleasant to have a family misfortune like this noised abroad. Besides, it is a useless expense, for how could you possibly find this Hosmer Angel?'

'On the contrary,' said Holmes quietly; 'I have every reason to believe that I will succeed in discovering Mr Hosmer Angel.'

Mr Windibank gave a violent start and dropped his gloves. 'I am delighted to hear it,' he said.

'It is a curious thing,' remarked Holmes, 'that a typewriter has really quite as much individuality as a man's handwriting. Unless they are quite new, no two of them write exactly alike. Some letters get more worn than others, and some wear only on one side. Now, you remark in this note of yours, Mr Windibank, that in every case there is some little slurring over of the "e," and a slight defect in the tail of the "r." There are fourteen other characteristics, but those are the more obvious.'

'We do all our correspondence with this machine at the office, and no doubt it is a little worn,' our visitor answered. glancing keenly at Holmes with his bright little eyes.

'And now I will show you what is really a very interesting study, Mr Windibank,' Holmes continued. 'I think of writing another little monograph some of these days on the typewriter and its relation to crime. It is a subject to which I have devoted some little attention. I have here four letters which purport to come from the missing man. They are all typewritten. In each case, not only are the "e's" slurred and the "r's" tailless, but you will observe, if you care to use my magnifying lens, that the fourteen other characteristics to which I have alluded are there as well.'

Mr Windibank sprang out of his chair and picked up his hat. 'I cannot waste time over this sort of fantastic talk, Mr Holmes,' he said. 'If you can catch the man, catch him, and let me know when you have done it.'

'Certainly,' said Holmes, stepping over and turning the key in the door. 'I let you know, then, that I have caught him!'

'What! Where?' shouted Mr Windibank, turning white to his lips and glancing about him like a rat in a trap.

'Oh, it won't do—really it won't,' said Holmes suavely. 'There is no possible getting out of it, Mr Windibank. It is quite too transparent, and it was a very bad compliment when you said that it was impossible for me to solve so simple a question. That's right! Sit down and let us talk it over.'

Our visitor collapsed into a chair, with a ghastly face and a glitter of moisture on his brow. 'It—it's not actionable,' he stammered.

'I am very much afraid that it is not. But between ourselves, Windibank, it was as cruel and selfish and heartless a trick in a petty way as ever came before me. Now, let me just run over the course of events, and you will contradict me if I go wrong.'

The man sat huddled up in his chair, with his head sunk upon his breast, like one who is utterly crushed. Holmes stuck his feet up on the corner of the mantelpiece and leaning back with his hands in his pockets, began talking, rather to himself, as it seemed, than to us.

'The man married a woman very much older than himself for her money,' said he, 'and he enjoyed the use of the money of the daughter as long as she lived with them. It was a considerable sum, for people in their position, and the loss of it would have made a serious difference. It was worth an effort to preserve it. The daughter was of a good, amiable disposition, but affectionate and warm-hearted in her ways. So that it was evident that with her fair personal advantages, and her little income, she would not be allowed to remain single long. Now her marriage would mean, of course, the loss of a hundred a year, so what does her stepfather do to prevent it? He takes the obvious course of keeping her at home and forbidding her to seek the company of people of her own age. But soon he found that that would not answer forever. She became restive, insisted upon her rights, and finally announced her positive intention of going to a certain ball. What does her clever stepfather do then? He conceives an idea more creditable to his head than to his heart. With the connivance and assistance of his wife he disguised himself, covered those keen eyes with tinted glasses, masked the face with a moustache and a pair of bushy whiskers, sunk that clear voice into an insinuating whisper, and doubly secure on account of the girl's short sight, he appears as Mr Hosmer Angel, and keeps off other lovers by making love himself.'

'It was only a joke at first,' groaned our visitor. 'We never thought that she would have been so carried away.'

'Very likely not. However that may be, the young lady was very decidedly carried away, and, having quite made up her mind that her stepfather was in France, the suspicion of treachery never for an instant entered her mind. She was flattered by the gentleman's attentions, and the effect was increased by the loudly expressed admiration of her mother. Then Mr Angel began to call, for it was obvious that the matter should be pushed as far as it would go if a real effect were to be produced. There were meetings, and an engagement, which would finally secure the girl's affections from turning towards anyone else. But the deception could not be kept up forever. These pretended journeys to France were rather cumbrous. The thing to do was clearly to bring the business to an end in such a dramatic manner that it would leave a permanent impression upon the young lady's mind and prevent her from looking upon any other suitor for some time to come.

Hence those vows of fidelity exacted upon a Testament, and hence also the allusions to a possibility of something happening on the very morning of the wedding. James Windibank wished Miss Sutherland to be so bound to Hosmer Angel, and so uncertain as to his fate, that for ten years to come, at any rate, she would not listen to another man. As far as the church door he brought her, and then, as he could go no farther, he conveniently vanished away by the old trick of stepping in at one door of a four-wheeler and out at the other. I think that was the chain of events, Mr Windibank!'

Our visitor had recovered something of his assurance while Holmes had been talking, and he rose from his chair now with a cold sneer upon his pale face.

'It may be so, or it may not. Mr Holmes,' said he. 'but if you are so very sharp you ought to be sharp enough to know that it is you who are breaking the law now, and not me. I have done nothing actionable from the first, but as long as you keep that door locked you lay yourself open to an action for assault and illegal constraint.'

'The law cannot, as you say, touch you,' said Holmes, unlocking and throwing open the door, 'yet there never was a man who deserved punishment more. If the young lady has a brother or a friend, he ought to lay a whip across your shoulders. By Jove!' he continued, flushing up at the sight of the bitter sneer upon the man's face, 'it is not part of my duties to my client, but here's a hunting crop handy, and I think I shall just treat myself to --' He took two swift steps to the whip, but before he could grasp it there was a wild clatter of steps upon the stairs, the heavy hall door banged, and from the window we could see Mr James Windibank running at the top of his speed down the road.

'There's a cold-blooded scoundrel!' said Holmes, laughing, as he threw himself down into his chair once more. 'That fellow will rise from crime to crime until he does something very bad, and ends on a gallows. The case has, in some respects, been not entirely devoid of interest.'

'I cannot now entirely see all the steps of your reasoning,' I remarked.

'Well, of course it was obvious from the first that this Mr Hosmer Angel must have some strong object for his curious conduct, and it was equally clear that the only man who really profited by the incident, as far as we could see, was the stepfather. Then the fact that the two men were never together, but that the one always appeared when the other was away, was suggestive. So were the tinted spectacles and the curious voice, which both hinted at a disguise, as did the bushy whiskers. My suspicions were all confirmed by his peculiar action in typewriting his signature, which, of course, inferred that his handwriting was so familiar to her that she would recognize even the smallest sample of it. You see all these isolated facts, together with many minor ones, all pointed in the same direction.'

'And how did you verify them?'

'Having once spotted my man, it was easy to get corroboration. I knew the firm for which this man worked. Having taken the printed description. I eliminated everything from it which could be the result of a disguise—the whiskers, the glasses, the voice, and I sent it to the firm, with a request that they would inform me whether it answered to the description of any of their travellers. I had already noticed the peculiarities of the typewriter, and I wrote to the man himself at his business address asking him if he would come here. As I expected, his reply was typewritten and revealed the same trivial but characteristic defects. The same post brought me a letter from Westhouse & Marbank, of Fenchurch Street, to say that the description tallied in every respect with that of their employee, James Windibank. Voila tout!'

'And Miss Sutherland?'

'If I tell her she will not believe me. You may remember

the old Persian saying, "There is danger for him who taketh the tiger cub, and danger also for whoso snatches a delusion from a woman." There is as much sense in Hafiz as in Horace, and as much knowledge of the world.'

3

THE ADVENTURE OF
THE SPECKLED BAND

On glancing over my notes of the seventy odd cases in which I have during the last eight years studied the methods of my friend Sherlock Holmes, I find many tragic, some comic, a large number merely strange, but none commonplace; for, working as he did rather for the love of his art than for the acquirement of wealth, he refused to associate himself with any investigation which did not tend towards the unusual, and even the fantastic. Of all these varied cases, however, I cannot recall any which presented more singular features than that which was associated with the well-known Surrey family of the Roylotts of Stoke Moran. The events in question occurred in the early days of my association with Holmes, when we were sharing rooms as bachelors in Baker Street. It is possible that I might have placed them upon record before, but a promise of secrecy was made at the time, from which I have only been freed during the last month by the untimely death of the lady to whom the pledge was given. It is perhaps as well that the facts should now come to light, for I have reasons to know that there are widespread rumours as to the death of Dr. Grimesby Roylott which tend to make the matter even more terrible than the truth.

It was early in April in the year '83 that I woke one morning to find Sherlock Holmes standing, fully dressed, by the side of my bed. He was a late riser, as a rule, and as the clock on the mantelpiece showed me that it was only a quarter-past seven, I blinked up at him in some surprise, and perhaps just a little resentment, for I was myself regular in my habits.

'Very sorry to knock you up, Watson,' said he, 'but it's the common lot this morning. Mrs Hudson has been knocked up, she retorted upon me, and I on you.'

'What is it, then—a fire?'

'No; a client. It seems that a young lady has arrived in a considerable state of excitement, who insists upon seeing me. She is waiting now in the sitting-room. Now, when young ladies wander about the metropolis at this hour of the morning, and knock sleepy people up out of their beds, I presume that it is something very pressing which they have to communicate. Should it prove to be an interesting case, you would, I am sure, wish to follow it from the outset. I thought, at any rate, that I should call you and give you the chance.'

'My dear fellow, I would not miss it for anything.'

I had no keener pleasure than in following Holmes in his professional investigations, and in admiring the rapid deductions, as swift as intuitions, and yet always founded on a logical basis with which, he unravelled the problems which were submitted to him. I rapidly threw on my clothes and was ready in a few minutes to accompany my friend down to the sitting-room. A lady dressed in black and heavily veiled, who had been sitting in the window, rose as we entered.

'Good-morning, madam,' said Holmes cheerily. 'My name is Sherlock Holmes. This is my intimate friend and associate, Dr. Watson, before whom you can speak as freely as before myself. Ha! I am glad to see that Mrs Hudson has had the good sense to light the fire. Pray draw up to it, and I shall order you a cup of hot coffee, for I observe that you are shivering.'

'It is not cold which makes me shiver,' said the woman in a low voice, changing her seat as requested.

'What, then?'

'It is fear, Mr Holmes. It is terror.' She raised her veil as she spoke, and we could see that she was indeed in a pitiable state of agitation, her face all drawn and gray, with restless frightened eyes like those of some hunted animal. Her features and figure were those of a woman of thirty, but her hair was shot with premature gray, and her expression was weary and haggard. Sherlock Holmes ran her over with one of his quick, all-comprehensive glances.

'You must not fear,' said he soothingly, bending forward and patting her forearm. 'We shall soon set matters right, I have no doubt. You have come in by train this morning, I see.'

'You know me, then?'

'No, but I observe the second half of a return ticket in the palm of your left glove. You must have started early, and yet you had a good drive in a dog-cart, along eavy roads, before you reached the station.'

The lady gave a violent start and stared in bewilderment at my companion.

'There is no mystery, my dear madam,' said he, smiling. 'The left arm of your jacket is spattered with mud in no less than seven places. The marks are perfectly fresh. There is no vehicle save a dog-cart which throws up mud in that way, and then only when you sit on the left-hand side of the driver.'

'Whatever your reasons may be, you are perfectly correct,' said she. 'I started from home before six, reached Leatherhead at twenty past, and came in by the first train to Waterloo. Sir, I can stand this strain no longer; I shall go mad if it continues. I have no one to turn to—none, save only one, who cares for me, and he, poor fellow, can be of little aid. I have heard of you, Mr Holmes; I have heard of you from Mrs Farintosh, whom you helped in the hour of her sore need. It was from her that I had your address. Oh, sir, do you not think that you could help me, too, and at least throw a little light through the dense darkness which surrounds me? At present it is out of my power to reward you for your services, but in a month or six weeks I shall be married, with the control of my own income, and then at least you shall not find me ungrateful.'

Holmes turned to his desk and, unlocking it, drew out a small case-book, which he consulted.

'Farintosh,' said he. 'Ah yes, I recall the case; it was concerned with an opal tiara. I think it was before your time, Watson. I can only say, madam, that I shall be happy to devote the same care to your case as I did to that of your friend. As to reward, my profession is its own reward; but you are at liberty to defray whatever expenses I may be put to, at the time which suits you best. And now I beg that you will lay before us everything that may help us in forming an opinion upon the matter.'

'Alas!' replied our visitor, 'the very horror of my situation lies in the fact that my fears are so vague, and my suspicions depend so entirely upon small points, which might seem trivial to another, that even he to whom of all others I have a right to look for help and advice looks upon all that I tell him about it as the fancies of a nervous woman. He does not say so, but I can read it from his soothing answers and averted eyes. But I have heard, Mr Holmes, that you can see deeply into the manifold wickedness of the human heart. You may advise me how to walk amid the dangers which encompass me.'

'I am all attention, madam.'

'My name is Helen Stoner, and I am living with my stepfather, who is the last survivor of one of the oldest Saxon families in England, the Roylotts of Stoke Moran, on the western border of Surrey.'

Holmes nodded his head. 'The name is familiar to me,' said he.

'The family was at one time among the richest in England,

and the estates extended over the borders into Berkshire in the north, and Hampshire in the west. In the last century, however, four successive heirs were of a dissolute and wasteful disposition, and the family ruin was eventually completed by a gambler in the days of the Regency. Nothing was left save a few acres of ground, and the two-hundred-year-old house, which is itself crushed under a heavy mortgage. The last squire dragged out his existence there, living the horrible life of an aristocratic pauper; but his only son, my stepfather, seeing that he must adapt himself to the new conditions, obtained an advance from a relative, which enabled him to take a medical degree and went out to Calcutta, where, by his professional skill and his force of character, he established a large practice. In a fit of anger, however, caused by some robberies which had been perpetrated in the house, he beat his native butler to death and narrowly escaped a capital sentence. As it was, he suffered a long term of imprisonment and afterwards returned to England a morose and disappointed man.

'When Dr. Roylott was in India he married my mother, Mrs Stoner, the young widow of Major-General Stoner, of the Bengal Artillery. My sister Julia and I were twins, and we were only two years old at the time of my mother's re-marriage. She had a considerable sum of money—not less than £1000 a year—and this she bequeathed to Dr. Roylott entirely while we resided with him, with a provision that a certain annual sum should be allowed to each of us in the event of our marriage. Shortly after our return to England my mother died—she was killed eight years ago in a railway accident near Crewe. Dr. Roylott then abandoned his attempts to establish himself in practice in London and took us to live with him in the old ancestral house at Stoke Moran. The money which my mother had left was enough for all our wants, and there seemed to be no obstacle to our happiness.

'But a terrible change came over our stepfather about this time. Instead of making friends and exchanging visits with our neighbours, who had at first been overjoyed to see a Roylott of Stoke Moran back in the old family seat, he shut himself up in his house and seldom came out save to indulge in ferocious quarrels with whoever might cross his path. Violence of temper approaching to mania has been hereditary in the men of the family, and in my stepfather's case it had, I believe, been intensified by his long residence in the tropics. A series of disgraceful brawls took place, two of which ended in the policecourt, until at last he became the terror of the village, and the folks would fly at his approach, for he is a man of immense strength, and absolutely uncontrollable in his anger.

'Last week he hurled the local blacksmith over a parapet into a stream, and it was only by paying over all the money which I could gather together that I was able to avert another public exposure. He had no friends at all save the wandering gypsies, and he would give these vagabonds leave to encamp upon the few acres of bramble-covered land which represent the family estate, and would accept in return the hospitality of their tents, wandering away with them sometimes for weeks on end. He has a passion also for Indian animals, which are sent over to him by a correspondent, and he has at this moment a cheetah and a baboon, which wander freely over his grounds and are feared by the villagers almost as much as their master.

'You can imagine from what I say that my poor sister Julia and I had no great pleasure in our lives. No servant would stay with us, and for a long time we did all the work of the house. She was but thirty at the time of her death, and yet her hair had already begun to whiten, even as mine has.'

'Your sister is dead, then?'

'She died just two years ago, and it is of her death that I wish to speak to you. You can understand that, living the life which I have described, we were little likely to see anyone of our own age and position. We had, however, an aunt, my mother's maiden sister, Miss Honoria Westphail, who lives near Harrow, and we were occasionally allowed to pay short visits at this lady's house. Julia went there at Christmas two years ago, and met there a half-pay major of marines, to whom she became engaged. My stepfather learned of the engagement when my sister returned and offered no objection to the marriage; but within a fortnight of the day which had been fixed for the wedding, the terrible event occurred which has deprived me of my only companion.'

Sherlock Holmes had been leaning back in his chair with his eyes closed and his head sunk in a cushion, but he half opened his lids now and glanced across at his visitor.

'Pray be precise as to details,' said he.

'It is easy for me to be so, for every event of that dreadful time is seared into my memory. The manor-house is, as I have already said, very old, and only one wing is now inhabited. The bedrooms in this wing are on the ground floor, the sitting-rooms being in the central block of the buildings. Of these bedrooms the first is Dr. Roylott's, the second my sister's, and the third my own. There is no communication between them, but they all open out into the same corridor. Do I make myself plain?'

'Perfectly so.'

'The windows of the three rooms open out upon the lawn. That fatal night Dr. Roylott had gone to his room early, though we knew that he had not retired to rest, for my sister was troubled by the smell of the strong Indian cigars which it was his custom to smoke. She left her room, therefore, and came into mine, where she sat for some time, chatting about her approaching wedding. At eleven o'clock she rose to leave me, but she paused at the door and looked back.

'"Tell me, Helen," said she, "have you ever heard anyone whistle in the dead of the night?"

'"Never," said I.

'"I suppose that you could not possibly whistle, yourself, in your sleep?"

'"Certainly not. But why?"

'"Because during the last few nights I have always, about three in the morning, heard a low, clear whistle. I am a light sleeper, and it has awakened me. I cannot tell where it came from perhaps from the next room, perhaps from the lawn. I thought that I would just ask you whether you had heard it."

'"No, I have not. It must be those wretched gypsies in the plantation."

'"Very likely. And yet if it were on the lawn, I wonder that you did not hear it also."

'"Ah, but I sleep more heavily than you."

'"Well, it is of no great consequence, at any rate." She smiled back at me, closed my door, and a few moments later I heard her key turn in the lock.'

'Indeed,' said Holmes. 'Was it your custom always to lock yourselves in at night?'

'Always.'

'And why?'

'I think that I mentioned to you that the doctor kept a cheetah and a baboon. We had no feeling of security unless our doors were locked.'

'Quite so. Pray proceed with your statement.'

'I could not sleep that night. A vague feeling of impending misfortune impressed me. My sister and I, you will recollect, were twins, and you know how subtle are the links which bind two souls which are so closely allied. It was a wild night. The wind was howling outside, and the rain was beating and splashing against the windows. Suddenly, amid all the hubbub of the gale, there burst forth the wild scream of a terrified woman. I knew that it was my sister's voice. I sprang from my bed, wrapped a shawl round me, and rushed into the corridor. As I opened my door I seemed to hear a low whistle, such as my sister described, and a few moments later a clanging sound, as if a mass of metal had fallen. As I ran down the passage, my sister's door was unlocked, and revolved slowly upon its hinges. I stared at it horror-stricken, not knowing what was about to issue from it. By the light of the corridor-lamp I saw my sister appear at the opening, her face blanched with terror, her hands groping for help, her whole figure swaying to and fro like that of a drunkard. I ran to her and threw my arms round her, but at that moment her knees seemed to give way and she fell to the ground. She writhed as one who is in terrible pain, and her limbs were dreadfully convulsed. At first I thought that she had not recognized me, but as I bent over her she suddenly shrieked out in a voice which I shall never forget, "Oh, my God! Helen! It was the band! The speckled band!" There was something else which she would fain have said, and she stabbed with her finger into the air in the direction of the doctor's room, but a fresh convulsion seized her and choked her words. I rushed out, calling loudly for my stepfather, and I met him hastening from his room in his dressing-gown. When he reached my sister's side she was unconscious, and though he poured brandy down her throat and sent for medical aid from the village, all efforts were in vain, for she slowly sank and died without having recovered her consciousness. Such was the dreadful end of my beloved sister.'

'One moment,' said Holmes, 'are you sure about this whistle and metallic sound? Could you swear to it?'

'That was what the county coroner asked me at the inquiry. It is my strong impression that I heard it, and yet, among the crash of the gale and the creaking of an old house, I may possibly have been deceived.'

'Was your sister dressed?'

'No, she was in her night-dress. In her right hand was found the charred stump of a match, and in her left a match-box.'

'Showing that she had struck a light and looked about her when the alarm took place. That is important. And what conclusions did the coroner come to?'

'He investigated the case with great care, for Dr. Roylott's conduct had long been notorious in the county, but he was unable to find any satisfactory cause of death. My evidence showed that the door had been fastened upon the inner side, and the windows were blocked by old-fashioned shutters with broad iron bars, which were secured every night. The walls were carefully sounded, and were shown to be quite solid all round, and the flooring was also thoroughly examined, with the same result. The chimney is wide, but is barred up by four large staples. It is certain, therefore, that my sister was quite alone when she met her end. Besides, there were no marks of any violence upon her.'

'How about poison?'

'The doctors examined her for it, but without success.'

'What do you think that this unfortunate lady died of, then?'

'It is my belief that she died of pure fear and nervous shock, though what it was that frightened her I cannot imagine.'

'Were there gypsies in the plantation at the time?'

'Yes, there are nearly always some there.'

'Ah, and what did you gather from this allusion to a band—a speckled band?'

'Sometimes I have thought that it was merely the wild talk of delirium, sometimes that it may have referred to some band of people, perhaps to these very gypsies in the plantation. I do not know whether the spotted handkerchiefs which so many of them wear over their heads might have suggested the strange adjective which she used.'

Holmes shook his head like a man who is far from being satisfied.

'These are very deep waters,' said he; 'pray go on with your narrative.'

'Two years have passed since then, and my life has been until lately lonelier than ever. A month ago, however, a dear friend, whom I have known for many years, has done me the honour to ask my hand in marriage. His name is Armitage—Percy Armitage—the second son of Mr Armitage, of Crane Water, near Reading. My stepfather has offered no opposition to the match, and we are to be married in the course of the spring. Two days ago some repairs were started in the west wing of the building, and my bedroom wall has been pierced, so that I have had to move into the chamber in which my sister died, and to sleep in the very bed in which she slept. Imagine, then, my thrill of terror when last night, as I lay awake, thinking over her terrible fate, I suddenly heard in the silence of the night the low whistle which had been the herald of her own death. I sprang up and lit the lamp, but nothing was to be seen in the room. I was too shaken to go to bed again, however, so I dressed, and as soon as it was daylight I slipped down, got a dog-cart at the Crown Inn, which is opposite, and drove to Leatherhead, from whence I have come on this morning with the one object of seeing you and asking your advice.'

'You have done wisely,' said my friend. 'But have you told me all?'

'Yes, all.'

'Miss Roylott, you have not. You are screening your stepfather.'

'Why, what do you mean?'

For answer Holmes pushed back the frill of black lace which fringed the hand that lay upon our visitor's knee. Five little livid spots, the marks of four fingers and a thumb, were printed upon the white wrist.

'You have been cruelly used,' said Holmes.

The lady coloured deeply and covered over her injured wrist. 'He is a hard man,' she said, 'and perhaps he hardly knows his own strength.'

There was a long silence, during which Holmes leaned his chin upon his hands and stared into the crackling fire.

'This is a very deep business,' he said at last. 'There are a thousand details which I should desire to know before I decide upon our course of action. Yet we have not a moment to lose. If we were to come to Stoke Moran today, would it be possible for us to see over these rooms without the knowledge of your stepfather?'

'As it happens, he spoke of coming into town today upon some most important business. It is probable that he will be away all day, and that there would be nothing to disturb you. We have a housekeeper now, but she is old and foolish, and I could easily get her out of the way.'

'Excellent. You are not averse to this trip, Watson?'

'By no means.'

'Then we shall both come. What are you going to do yourself?'

'I have one or two things which I would wish to do now that I am in town. But I shall return by the twelve o'clock train, so as to be there in time for your coming.'

'And you may expect us early in the afternoon. I have myself some small business matters to attend to. Will you not wait and breakfast?'

'No, I must go. My heart is lightened already since I have confided my trouble to you. I shall look forward to seeing you again this afternoon.' She dropped her thick black veil over her face and glided from the room.

'And what do you think of it all, Watson?' asked Sherlock Holmes, leaning back in his chair.

'It seems to me to be a most dark and sinister business.'

'Dark enough and sinister enough.'

'Yet if the lady is correct in saying that the flooring and walls are sound, and that the door, window, and chimney are impassable, then her sister must have been undoubtedly alone when she met her mysterious end.'

'What becomes, then, of these nocturnal whistles, and what of the very peculiar words of the dying woman?'

'I cannot think.'

'When you combine the ideas of whistles at night, the

presence of a band of gypsies who are on intimate terms with this old doctor, the fact that we have every reason to believe that the doctor has an interest in preventing his stepdaughter's marriage, the dying allusion to a band, and, finally, the fact that Miss Helen Stoner heard a metallic clang, which might have been caused by one of those metal bars that secured the shutters falling back into its place, I think that there is good ground to think that the mystery may be cleared along those lines.'

'But what, then, did the gypsies do?'

'I cannot imagine.'

'I see many objections to any such theory.'

'And so do I. It is precisely for that reason that we are going to Stoke Moran this day. I want to see whether the objections are fatal, or if they may be explained away. But what in the name of the devil!'

The ejaculation had been drawn from my companion by the fact that our door had been suddenly dashed open, and that a huge man had framed himself in the aperture. His costume was a peculiar mixture of the professional and of the agricultural, having a black top-hat, a long frock-coat, and a pair of high gaiters, with a hunting-crop swinging in his hand. So tall was he that his hat actually brushed the cross bar of the doorway, and his breadth seemed to span it across from side to side. A large face, seared with a thousand wrinkles, burned yellow with the sun, and marked with every evil passion, was turned from one to the other of us, while his deep-set, bile-shot eyes, and his high, thin, fleshless nose, gave him somewhat the resemblance to a fierce old bird of prey.

'Which of you is Holmes?' asked this apparition.

'My name, sir; but you have the advantage of me,' said my companion quietly.

'I am Dr. Grimesby Roylott, of Stoke Moran.'

'Indeed, Doctor,' said Holmes blandly. 'Pray take a seat.'

'I will do nothing of the kind. My stepdaughter has been here.

I have traced her. What has she been saying to you?'

'It is a little cold for the time of the year,' said Holmes.

'What has she been saying to you?' screamed the old man furiously.

'But I have heard that the crocuses promise well,' continued my companion imperturbably.

'Ha! You put me off, do you?' said our new visitor, taking a step forward and shaking his hunting-crop. 'I know you, you scoundrel! I have heard of you before. You are Holmes, the meddler.'

My friend smiled.

'Holmes, the busybody!'

His smile broadened.

'Holmes, the Scotland Yard Jack-in-office!'

Holmes chuckled heartily. 'Your conversation is most entertaining,' said he. 'When you go out close the door, for there is a decided draught.'

'I will go when I have said my say. Don't you dare to meddle with my affairs. I know that Miss Stoner has been here. I traced her! I am a dangerous man to fall foul of! See here.' He stepped swiftly forward, seized the poker, and bent it into a curve with his huge brown hands.

'See that you keep yourself out of my grip,' he snarled, and hurling the twisted poker into the fireplace he strode out of the room.

'He seems a very amiable person,' said Holmes, laughing. 'I am not quite so bulky, but if he had remained I might have shown him that my grip was not much more feeble than his own.' As he spoke he picked up the steel poker and, with a sudden effort, straightened it out again.

'Fancy his having the insolence to confound me with the official detective force! This incident gives zest to our investigation, however, and I only trust that our little friend will not suffer from her imprudence in allowing this brute to trace her. And now,

Watson, we shall order breakfast, and afterwards I shall walk down to Doctors' Commons, where I hope to get some data which may help us in this matter.'

It was nearly one o'clock when Sherlock Holmes returned from his excursion. He held in his hand a sheet of blue paper, scrawled over with notes and figures.

'I have seen the will of the deceased wife,' said he. 'To determine its exact meaning I have been obliged to work out the present prices of the investments with which it is concerned. The total income, which at the time of the wife's death was little short of £1100, is now, through the fall in agricultural prices, not more than £750. Each daughter can claim an income of £250, in case of marriage. It is evident, therefore, that if both girls had married, this beauty would have had a mere pittance, while even one of them would cripple him to a very serious extent. My morning's work has not been wasted, since it has proved that he has the very strongest motives for standing in the way of anything of the sort. And now, Watson, this is too serious for dawdling, especially as the old man is aware that we are interesting ourselves in his affairs; so if you are ready, we shall call a cab and drive to Waterloo. I should be very much obliged if you would slip your revolver into your pocket. An Eley's No. 2 is an excellent argument with gentlemen who can twist steel pokers into knots. That and a tooth-brush are, I think all that we need.'

At Waterloo we were fortunate in catching a train for Leatherhead, where we hired a trap at the station inn and drove for four or five miles through the lovely Surrey laries. It was a perfect day, with a bright sun and a few fleecy clouds in the heavens. The trees and wayside hedges were just throwing out their first green shoots, and the air was full of the pleasant smell of the moist earth. To me at least there was a strange contrast between the sweet promise of the spring and this sinister quest upon which we were engaged. My companion sat in the front of the trap, his arms folded, his hat pulled down over his eyes, and his chin sunk upon his breast, buried in the deepest thought. Suddenly, however, he started, tapped me on the shoulder, and pointed over the meadows.

'Look there!' said he.

A heavily timbered park stretched up in a gentle slope, thickening into a grove at the highest point. From amid the branches there jutted out the gray gables and high roof-tree of a very old mansion.

'Stoke Moran?' said he.

'Yes, sir, that be the house of Dr. Grimesby Roylott,' remarked the driver.

'There is some building going on there,' said Holmes; 'that is where we are going.'

'There's the village,' said the driver, pointing to a cluster of roofs some distance to the left; 'but if you want to get to the house, you'll find it shorter to get over this stile, and so by the footpath over the fields. There it is, where the lady is walking.'

'And the lady, I fancy, is Miss Stoner,' observed Holmes, shading his eyes. 'Yes, I think we had better do as you suggest.'

We got off, paid our fare, and the trap rattled back on its way to Leatherhead.

'I thought it as well,' said Holmes as we climbed the stile, 'that this fellow should think we had come here as architects, or on some definite business. It may stop his gossip. Good-afternoon, Miss Stoner. You see that we have been as good as our word.'

Our client of the morning had hurried forward to meet us with a face which spoke her joy. 'I have been waiting so eagerly for you,' she cried, shaking hands with us warmly. 'All has turned out splendidly. Dr. Roylott has gone to town, and it is unlikely that he will be back before evening.'

'We have had the pleasure of making the doctor's acquaintance,' said Holmes, and in a few words he sketched out what had occurred. Miss Stoner turned white to the lips as she listened.

'Good heavens!' she cried, 'he has followed me, then.'

'So it appears.'

'He is so cunning that I never know when I am safe from him. What will he say when he returns?'

'He must guard himself, for he may find that there is someone more cunning than himself upon his track. You must lock yourself up from him tonight. If he is violent, we shall take you away to your aunt's at Harrow. Now, we must make the best use of our time, so kindly take us at once to the rooms which we are to examine.'

The building was of gray, lichen-blotched stone, with a high central portion and two curving wings, like the claws of a crab, thrown out on each side. In one of these wings the windows were broken and blocked with wooden boards, while the roof was partly caved in, a picture of ruin. The central portion was in little better repair, but the right-hand block was comparatively modern, and the blinds in the windows, with the blue smoke curling up from the chimneys, showed that this was where the family resided. Some scaffolding had been erected against the end wall, and the stone-work had been broken into, but there were no signs of any workmen at the moment of our visit. Holmes walked slowly up and down the ill-trimmed lawn and examined with deep attention the outsides of the windows.

'This, I take it, belongs to the room in which you used to sleep, the centre one to your sister's, and the one next to the main building to Dr. Roylott's chamber?'

'Exactly so. But I am now sleeping in the middle one.'

'Pending the alterations, as I understand. By the way, there does not seem to be any very pressing need for repairs at that end wall.'

'There were none. I believe that it was an excuse to move me from my room.'

'Ah! That is suggestive. Now, on the other side of this narrow wing runs the corridor from which these three rooms open. There are windows in it, of course?' 'Yes, but very small ones. Too narrow for anyone to pass through.'

'As you both locked your doors at night, your rooms were unapproachable from that side. Now, would you have the kindness to go into your room and bar your shutters?'

Miss Stoner did so, and Holmes, after a careful examination through the open window, endeavoured in every way to force the shutter open, but without success. There was no slit through which a knife could be passed to raise the bar. Then with his lens he tested the hinges, but they were of solid iron, built firmly into the massive masonry. 'Hum!' said he, scratching his chin in some perplexity, 'my theory certainly presents some difficulties. No one could pass these shutters if they were bolted. Well, we shall see if the inside throws any light upon the matter.'

A small side door led into the whitewashed corridor from which the three bedrooms opened. Holmes refused to examine the third chamber, so we passed at once to the second, that in which Miss Stoner was now sleeping, and in which her sister had met with her fate. It was a homely little room, with a low ceiling and a gaping fireplace, after the fashion of old country-houses. A brown chest of drawers stood in one corner, a narrow white-counterpaned bed in another, and a dressing-table on the left-hand side of the window. These articles, with two small wicker-work chairs, made up all the furniture in the room save for a square of Wilton carpet in the centre. The boards round and the panelling of the walls were of brown, worm-eaten oak, so old and discoloured that it may have dated from the original building of the house. Holmes drew one of the chairs into a corner and sat silent, while his eyes travelled round and round and up and down, taking in every detail of the apartment.

'Where does that bell communicate with?' he asked, at last, pointing to a thick belt-rope which hung down beside the bed, the tassel actually lying upon the pillow.

'It goes to the housekeeper's room.'

'It looks newer than the other things?'

'Yes, it was only put there a couple of years ago.'

'Your sister asked for it, I suppose?'

'No, I never heard of her using it. We used always to get what we wanted for ourselves.'

'Indeed, it seemed unnecessary to put so nice a bell-pull there. You will excuse me for a few minutes while I satisfy myself as to this floor.' He threw himself down upon his face with his lens in his hand and crawled swiftly backward and forward, examining minutely the cracks between the boards. Then he did the same with the wood-work with which the chamber was panelled. Finally he walked over to the bed and spent some time in staring at it and in running his eye up and down the wall. Finally he took the bell-rope in his hand and gave it a brisk tug.

'Why, it's a dummy,' said he.

'Won't it ring?'

'No, it is not even attached to a wire. This is very interesting. You can see now that it is fastened to a hook just above where the little opening for the ventilator is.'

'How very absurd! I never noticed that before.'

'Very strange!' muttered Holmes, pulling at the rope. 'There are one or two very singular points about this room. For example, what a fool a builder must be to open a ventilator into another room, when, with the same trouble, he might have communicated with the outside air!'

'That is also quite modern,' said the lady.

'Done about the same time as the bell-rope?' remarked Holmes.

'Yes, there were several little changes carried out about that time.'

'They seem to have been of a most interesting character—

dummy bell-ropes, and ventilators which do not ventilate. With your permission, Miss Stoner, we shall now carry our researches into the inner apartment.'

Dr. Grimesby Roylott's chamber was larger than that of his stepdaughter, but was as plainly furnished. A camp-bed, a small wooden shelf full of books, mostly of a technical character, an armchair beside the bed, a plain wooden chair against the wall, a round table, and a large iron safe, were the principal things which met the eye. Holmes walked slowly round and examined each and all of them with the keenest interest.

'What's in here?' he asked, tapping the safe.

'My stepfather's business papers.'

'Oh! You have seen inside, then?'

'Only once, some years ago. I remember that it was full of papers.'

'There isn't a cat in it, for example?'

'No. What a strange idea!'

'Well, look at this!' He took up a small saucer of milk which stood on the top of it.

'No, we don't keep a cat. But there is a cheetah and a baboon.'

'Ah, yes, of course! Well, a cheetah is just a big cat, and yet a saucer of milk does not go very far in satisfying its wants, I daresay. There is one point which I should wish to determine.' He squatted down in front of the wooden chair and examined the seat of it with the greatest attention.

'Thank you. That is quite settled,' said he, rising and putting his lens in his pocket. 'Hello! Here is something interesting!'

The object which had caught his eye was a small dog lash hung on one corner of the bed. The lash, however, was curled upon itself and tied so as to make a loop of whipcord.

'What do you make of that, Watson?'

'It's a common enough lash. But I don't know why if should be tied.'

'That is not quite so common, is it? Ah, me! It's a wicked world, and when a clever man turns his brains to crime it is the worst of all. I think that I have seen enough now, Miss Stoner, and with your permission we shall walk out upon the lawn.'

I had never seen my friend's face so grim or his brow so dark as it was when we turned from the scene of this investigation. We had walked several times up and down the lawn, neither Miss Stoner nor myself liking to break in upon his thoughts before he roused himself from his reverie.

'It is very essential, Miss Stoner,' said he, 'that you should absolutely follow my advice in every respect.'

'I shall most certainly do so.'

'The matter is too serious for any hesitation. Your life may depend upon your compliance.'

'I assure you that I am in your hands.'

'In the first place, both my friend and I must spend the night in your room.'

Both Miss Stoner and I gazed at him in astonishment.

'Yes, it must be so. Let me explain. I believe that that is the village inn over there?'

'Yes, that is the Crown.'

'Very good. Your windows would be visible from there?'

'Certainly.'

'You must confine yourself to your room, on pretence of a headache, when your stepfather comes back. Then when you hear him retire for the night, you must open the shutters of your window, undo the hasp, put your lamp there as a signal to us, and then withdraw quietly with everything which you are likely to want into the room which you used to occupy. I have no doubt that, in spite of the repairs, you could manage there for one night.'

'Oh, yes, easily.'

'The rest you will leave in our hands.'

'But what will you do?'

'We shall spend the night in your room, and we shall investigate the cause of this noise which has disturbed you.'

'I believe, Mr Holmes, that you have already made up your mind,' said Miss Stoner, laying her hand upon my companion's sleeve.

'Perhaps I have.'

'Then, for pity's sake, tell me what was the cause of my sister's death.'

'I should prefer to have clearer proofs before I speak.'

'You can at least tell me whether my own thought is correct, and if she died from some sudden fright.'

'No, I do not think so. I think that there was probably some more tangible cause. And now, Miss Stoner, we must leave you for if Dr. Roylott returned and saw us our journey would be in vain. Good-bye, and be brave, for if you will do what I have told you you may rest assured that we shall soon drive away the dangers that threaten you.'

Sherlock Holmes and I had no difficulty in engaging a bedroom and sitting-room at the Crown Inn. They were on the upper floor, and from our window we could command a view of the avenue gate, and of the inhabited wing of Stoke Moran Manor House. At dusk we saw Dr. Grimesby Roylott drive past, his huge form looming up beside the little figure of the lad who drove him. The boy had some slight difficulty in undoing the heavy iron gates, and we heard the hoarse roar of the doctor's voice and saw the fury with which he shook his clinched fists at him. The trap drove on, and a few minutes later we saw a sudden light spring up among the trees as the lamp was lit in one of the sitting-rooms.

'Do you know, Watson,' said Holmes as we sat together in the gathering darkness, 'I have really some scruples as to taking you tonight. There is a distinct element of danger.'

'Can I be of assistance?'

'Your presence might be invaluable.'

'Then I shall certainly come.'

'It is very kind of you.'

'You speak of danger. You have evidently seen more in these rooms than was visible to me.'

'No, but I fancy that I may have deduced a little more. I imagine that you saw all that I did.'

'I saw nothing remarkable save the bell-rope, and what purpose that could answer I confess is more than I can imagine.'

'You saw the ventilator, too?'

'Yes, but I do not think that it is such a very unusual thing to have a small opening between two rooms. It was so small that a rat could hardly pass through.'

'I knew that we should find a ventilator before ever we came to Stoke Moran.'

'My dear Holmes!'

'Oh, yes, I did. You remember in her statement she said that her sister could smell Dr. Roylott's cigar. Now, of course that suggested at once that there must be a communication between the two rooms. It could only be a small one, or it would have been remarked upon at the coroner's inquiry. I deduced a ventilator.'

'But what harm can there be in that?'

'Well, there is at least a curious coincidence of dates. A ventilator is made, a cord is hung, and a lady who sleeps in the bed dies. Does not that strike you?'

'I cannot as yet see any connection.'

'Did you observe anything very peculiar about that bed?'

'No.'

'It was clamped to the floor. Did you ever see a bed fastened like that before?'

'I cannot say that I have.'

'The lady could not move her bed. It must always be in the same relative position to the ventilator and to the rope—or so we may call it, since it was clearly never meant for a bell-pull.'

'Holmes,' I cried, 'I seem to see dimly what you are hinting at. We are only just in time to prevent some subtle and horrible crime.'

'Subtle enough and horrible enough. When a doctor does go wrong he is the first of criminals. He has nerve and he has knowledge. Palmer and Pritchard were among the heads of their profession. This man strikes even deeper, but I think, Watson, that we shall be able to strike deeper still. But we shall have horrors enough before the night is over; for goodness' sake let us have a quiet pipe and turn our minds for a few hours to something more cheerful.'

About nine o'clock the light among the trees was extinguished, and all was dark in the direction of the Manor House. Two hours passed slowly away, and then, suddenly, just at the stroke of eleven, a single bright light shone out right in front of us.

'That is our signal,' said Holmes, springing to his feet; 'it comes from the middle window.'

As we passed out he exchanged a few words with the landlord, explaining that we were going on a late visit to an acquaintance, and that it was possible that we might spend the night there. A moment later we were out on the dark road, a chill wind blowing in our faces, and one yellow light twinkling in front of us through the gloom to guide us on our sombre errand.

There was little difficulty in entering the grounds, for unrepaired breaches gaped in the old park wall. Making our way among the trees, we reached the lawn, crossed it, and were about to enter through the window when out from a clump of laurel bushes there darted what seemed to be a hideous and distorted child, who threw itself upon the grass with writhing limbs and then ran swiftly across the lawn into the darkness.

'My God!' I whispered; 'did you see it?'

Holmes was for the moment as startled as I. His hand closed like a vise upon my wrist in his agitation. Then he broke into a low laugh and put his lips to my ear.

'It is a nice household,' he murmured. 'That is the baboon.'

I had forgotten the strange pets which the doctor affected. There was a cheetah, too; perhaps we might find it upon our shoulders at any moment. I confess that I felt easier in my mind when, after following Holmes's example and slipping off my shoes, I found myself inside the bedroom. My companion noiselessly closed the shutters, moved the lamp onto the table, and cast his eyes round the room. All was as we had seen it in the daytime. Then creeping up to me and making a trumpet of his hand, he whispered into my ear again so gently that it was all that I could do to distinguish the words:

'The least sound would be fatal to our plans.'

I nodded to show that I had heard.

'We must sit without light. He would see it through the ventilator.'

I nodded again.

'Do not go asleep; your very life may depend upon it. Have your pistol ready in case we should need it. I will sit on the side of the bed, and you in that chair.'

I took out my revolver and laid it on the corner of the table.

Holmes had brought up a long thin cane, and this he placed upon the bed beside him. By it he laid the box of matches and the stump of a candle. Then he turned down the lamp, and we were left in darkness.

How shall I ever forget that dreadful vigil? I could not hear a sound, not even the drawing of a breath, and yet I knew that my companion sat open-eyed, within a few feet of me, in the same state of nervous tension in which I was myself. The shutters cut off the least ray of light, and we waited in absolute darkness. From outside came the occasional cry of a night-bird, and once at our very window a long drawn catlike whine, which told us that the cheetah was indeed at liberty. Far away we could hear the deep tones of the parish clock, which boomed out every quarter of an hour. How long they seemed, those quarters! Twelve struck, and one and two and three, and still we sat waiting silently for whatever might befall.

Suddenly there was the momentary gleam of a light up in the direction of the ventilator, which vanished immediately, but was succeeded by a strong smell of burning oil and heated metal. Someone in the next room had lit a dark-lantern. I heard a gentle sound of movement, and then all was silent once more, though the smell grew stronger. For half an hour I sat with straining ears. Then suddenly another sound became audible—a very gentle, soothing sound, like that of a small jet of steam escaping continually from a kettle. The instant that we heard it, Holmes sprang from the bed, struck a match, and lashed furiously with his cane at the bell-pull.

'You see it, Watson?' he yelled. 'You see it?'

But I saw nothing. At the moment when Holmes struck the light I heard a low, clear whistle, but the sudden glare flashing into my weary eyes made it impossible for me to tell what it was at which my friend lashed so savagely. I could, however, see that his face was deadly pale and filled with horror and loathing. He had ceased to strike and was gazing up at the ventilator when suddenly there broke from the silence of the night the most horrible cry to which I have ever listened. It swelled up louder and louder, a hoarse yell of pain and fear and anger all mingled in the one dreadful shriek. They say that away down in the village, and even in the distant parsonage, that cry raised the sleepers from their beds. It struck cold to our hearts, and I stood gazing at Holmes, and he at me, until the last echoes of it had died away into the silence from which it rose.

'What can it mean?' I gasped.

'It means that it is all over,' Holmes answered. 'And perhaps, after all, it is for the best. Take your pistol, and we will enter Dr.

Roylott's room.'

With a grave face he lit the lamp and led the way down the corridor. Twice he struck at the chamber door without any reply from within. Then he turned the handle and entered, I at his heels, with the cocked pistol in my hand.

It was a singular sight which met our eyes. On the table stood a dark-lantern with the shutter half open, throwing a brilliant beam of light upon the iron safe, the door of which was ajar. Beside this table, on the wooden chair, sat Dr. Grimesby Roylott clad in a long gray dressing-gown, his bare ankles protruding beneath, and his feet thrust into red heelless Turkish slippers. Across his lap lay the short stock with the long lash which we had noticed during the day. His chin was cocked upward and his eyes were fixed in a dreadful, rigid stare at the corner of the ceiling. Round his brow he had a peculiar yellow band, with brownish speckles, which seemed to be bound tightly round his head. As we entered he made neither sound nor motion.

'The band! the speckled band!' whispered Holmes.

I took a step forward. In an instant his strange headgear began to move, and there reared itself from among his hair the squat diamond-shaped head and puffed neck of a loathsome serpent.

'It is a swamp adder!' cried Holmes; 'the deadliest snake in India. He has died within ten seconds of being bitten. Violence does, in truth, recoil upon the violent, and the schemer falls into the pit which he digs for another. Let us thrust this creature back into its den, and we can then remove Miss Stoner to some place of shelter and let the county police know what has happened.'

As he spoke he drew the dog-whip swiftly from the dead man's lap, and throwing the noose round the reptile's neck he drew it from its horrid perch and, carrying it at arm's length, threw it into the iron safe, which he closed upon it.

Such are the true facts of the death of Dr. Grimesby Roylott, of Stoke Moran. It is not necessary that I should prolong a narrative which has already run to too great a length by telling how we broke the sad news to the terrified girl, how we conveyed her by the morning train to the care of her good aunt at Harrow, of how the slow process of official inquiry came to the conclusion that the doctor met his fate while indiscreetly playing with a dangerous pet. The little which I had yet to learn of the case was told me by Sherlock Holmes as we travelled back next day.

'I had,' said he, 'come to an entirely erroneous conclusion which shows, my dear Watson, how dangerous it always is to reason from insufficient data. The presence of the gypsies, and the use of the word 'band,' which was used by the poor girl, no doubt to explain the appearance which she had caught a hurried glimpse of by the light of her match, were sufficient to put me upon an entirely wrong scent. I can only claim the merit that I instantly reconsidered my position when, however, it became clear to me that whatever danger threatened an occupant of the room could not come either from the window or the door. My attention was speedily drawn, as I have already remarked to you, to this ventilator, and to the bell-rope which hung down to the bed. The discovery that this was a dummy, and that the bed was clamped to the floor, instantly gave rise to the suspicion that the rope was there as a bridge for something passing through the hole and coming to the bed. The idea of a snake instantly occurred to me, and when I coupled it with my knowledge that the doctor was furnished with a supply of creatures from India, I felt that I was probably on the right track. The idea of using a form of poison which could not possibly be discovered by any chemical test was just such a one as would occur to a clever and ruthless man who had had an Eastern training. The rapidity with which such a poison would take effect would also, from his point of view, be an advantage. It would be a sharp-eyed coroner, indeed, who could distinguish the two little dark punctures which would show where the poison fangs had done their work. Then I thought of the whistle. Of course he must recall the snake before the morning light revealed it to the victim. He had trained it, probably by the use of the milk which we saw, to return to him when summoned. He would put it through this ventilator at the hour that he thought best, with the certainty that it would crawl down the rope and land on the bed. It might or might not bite the occupant, perhaps she might escape every night for a week, but sooner or later she must fall a victim.

'I had come to these conclusions before ever I had entered his room. An inspection of his chair showed me that he had been in the habit of standing on it, which of course would be necessary in order that he should reach the ventilator. The sight of the safe, the saucer of milk, and the loop of whipcord were enough to finally dispel any doubts which may have remained. The metallic clang heard by Miss Stoner was obviously caused by her stepfather hastily closing the door of his safe upon its terrible occupant. Having once made up my mind, you know the steps which I took in order to put the matter to the proof. I heard the creature hiss as I have no doubt that you did also, and I instantly lit the light and attacked it.'

'With the result of driving it through the ventilator.'

'And also with the result of causing it to turn upon its master at the other side. Some of the blows of my cane came home and roused its snakish temper, so that it flew upon the first person it saw. In this way I am no doubt indirectly responsible for Dr. Grimesby Roylott's death, and I cannot say that it is likely to weigh very heavily upon my conscience.'

4

THE ADVENTURE OF
THE YELLOW FACE

Sherlock Holmes was a man who seldom took exercise for exercise's sake. Few men were capable of greater muscular effort, and he was undoubtedly one of the finest boxers of his weight that I have ever seen; but he looked upon aimless bodily exertion as a waste of energy, and he seldom bestirred himself save where there was some professional object to be served. Then he was absolutely untiring and indefatigable. That he should have kept himself in training under such circumstances is remarkable, but his diet was usually of the sparest, and his habits were simple to the verge of austerity. Save for the occasional use of cocaine, he had no vices, and he only turned to the drug as a protest against the monotony of existence when cases were scanty and the papers uninteresting.

One day in early spring he had so far relaxed as to go for a walk with me in the Park, where the first faint shoots of green were breaking out upon the elms, and the sticky spear-heads of the chestnuts were just beginning to burst into their five-fold leaves. For two hours we rambled about together, in silence for the most part, as befits two men who know each other intimately. It was nearly five before we were back in Baker Street once more.

'Beg pardon, sir,' said our page-boy as he opened the door. 'There's been a gentleman here asking for you, sir.'

Holmes glanced reproachfully at me. 'So much for afternoon walks!' said he. 'Has this gentleman gone, then?'

'Yes, sir.'

'Didn't you ask him in?'

'Yes, sir, he came in.'

'How long did he wait?'

'Half an hour, sir. He was a very restless gentleman, sir a-walkin' and a-stampin' all the time he was here. I was waitin' outside the door, sir, and I could hear him. At last he outs into the passage, and he cries, "Is that man never goin' to come?" Those were his very words, sir. "You'll only need to wait a little longer," says I. "Then I'll wait in the open air, for I feel half choked," says he. "I'll be back before long." And with that he ups and he outs, and all I could say wouldn't hold him back.'

'Well, well, you did your best,' said Holmes as we walked into our room. 'It's very annoying, though, Watson. I was badly in need of a case, and this looks, from the man's impatience, as if it were of importance. Hullo! That's not your pipe on the table. He must have left his behind him. A nice old brier with a good long stem of what the tobacconists call amber. I wonder how many real amber mouthpieces there are in London? Some people think that a fly in it is a sign. Well, he must have been disturbed in his mind to leave a pipe behind him which he evidently values highly.'

'How do you know that he values it highly?' I asked.

'Well, I should put the original cost of the pipe at seven and sixpence. Now it has, you see, been twice mended, once in the wooden stem and once in the amber. Each of these mends, done, as you observe, with silver bands, must have cost more than the pipe did originally. The man must value the pipe highly when he prefers to patch it up rather than buy a new one with the same money.'

'Anything else?' I asked, for Holmes was turning the pipe about in his hand and staring at it in his peculiar pensive way.

He held it up and tapped on it with his long, thin forefinger, as a professor might who was lecturing on a bone.

'Pipes are occasionally of extraordinary interest,' said he. 'Nothing has more individuality, save perhaps watches and bootlaces. The indications here, however, are neither very marked nor very important. The owner is obviously a muscular man, left-handed, with an excellent set of teeth, careless in his habits, and with no need to practise economy.'

My friend threw out the information in a very offhand way, but I saw that he cocked his eye at me to see if I had followed his reasoning.

'You think a man must be well-to-do if he smokes a seven-shilling pipe?' said I.

'This is Grosvenor mixture at eightpence an ounce,' Holmes answered, knocking a little out on his palm. 'As he might get an excellent smoke for half the price, he has no need to practise economy.'

'And the other points?'

'He has been in the habit of lighting his pipe at lamps and gasjets. You can see that it is quite charred all down one side. Of course a match could not have done that. Why should a man hold a match to the side of his pipe? But you cannot light it at a lamp without getting the bowl charred. And it is all on the right side of the pipe. From that I gather that he is a left-handed man. You hold your own pipe to the lamp and see how naturally you, being right-handed, hold the left side to the flame. You might do it once the other way, but not as a constancy. This has always been held so. Then he has bitten through his amber. It takes a muscular, energetic fellow, and one with a good set of teeth, to do that. But if I am not mistaken I hear him upon the stair, so we shall have something more interesting than his pipe to study.'

An instant later our door opened, and a tall young man entered the room. He was well but quietly dressed in a dark gray suit and carried a brown wideawake in his hand. I should have put him at about thirty, though he was really some years older.

'I beg your pardon,' said he with some embarrassment, 'I suppose I should have knocked. Yes, of course I should have knocked. The fact is that I am a little upset, and you must put it all down to that.' He passed his hand over his forehead like a man who is half dazed, and then fell rather than sat down upon a chair.

'I can see that you have not slept for a night or two,' said Holmes in his easy, genial way. 'That tries a man's nerves more than work, and more even than pleasure. May I ask how I can help you?'

'I wanted your advice, sir. I don't know what to do, and my whole life seems to have gone to pieces.'

'You wish to employ me as a consulting detective?'

'Not that only. I want your opinion as a judicious man—as a man of the world. I want to know what I ought to do next. I hope to God you'll be able to tell me.'

He spoke in little, sharp, jerky outbursts, and it seemed to me that to speak at all was very painful to him, and that his will all through was overriding his inclinations.

'It's a very delicate thing,' said he. 'One does not like to speak of one's domestic affairs to strangers. It seems dreadful to discuss the conduct of one's wife with two men whom I have never seen before. It's horrible to have to do it. But I've got to the end of my tether, and I must have advice.'

'My dear Mr Grant Munro—' began Holmes.

Our visitor sprang from his chair. 'What!' he cried, 'you know my name?'

'If you wish to preserve your incognito,' said Holmes, smiling, 'I would suggest that you cease to write your name upon the lining of your hat, or else that you turn the crown towards the person whom you are addressing. I was about to say that my friend and I have listened to a good many strange secrets in this room, and that we have had the good fortune to bring peace to many troubled souls. I trust that we may do as much for you. Might I beg you, as time may prove to be of importance, to furnish me with the facts of your case without further delay?'

Our visitor again passed his hand over his forehead, as if he found it bitterly hard. From every gesture and expression I could see that he was a reserved, self-contained man, with a dash of pride in his nature, more likely to hide his wounds than to expose them. Then suddenly, with a fierce gesture of his closed hand, like one who throws reserve to the winds, he began:

'The facts are these, Mr Holmes,' said he. 'I am a married man and have been so for three years. During that time my wife and I have loved each other as fondly and lived as happily as any two that ever were joined. We have not had a difference, not one, in thought or word or deed. And now, since last Monday, there has suddenly sprung up a barrier between us, and I find that there is something in her life and in her thoughts of which I know as little as if she were the woman who brushes by me in the street. We are estranged, and I want to know why.

'Now there is one thing that I want to impress upon you before I go any further, Mr Holmes. Effie loves me. Don't let there be any mistake about that. She loves me with her whole heart and soul, and never more than now. I know it. I feel it. I don't want to argue about that. A man can tell easily enough when a woman loves him. But there's this secret between us, and we can never be the same until it is cleared.'

'Kindly let me have the facts, Mr Munro,' said Holmes with some impatience.

'I'll tell you what I know about Effie's history. She was a widow when I met her first, though quite young—only twenty-five. Her name then was Mrs Hebron. She went out to America when she was young and lived in the town of Atlanta, where she married this Hebron, who was a lawyer with a good practice. They had one child, but the yellow fever broke out badly in the place, and both husband and child died of it. I have seen his death certificate. This sickened her of America, and she came back to live with a maiden aunt at Pinner, in Middlesex. I may mention that her husband had left her comfortably off, and that she had a capital of about four thousand five hundred pounds, which had been so well invested by him that it returned an average of seven per cent. She had only been six months at Pinner when I met her; we fell in love with each other, and we married a few weeks afterwards.

'I am a hop merchant myself, and as I have an income of seven or eight hundred, we found ourselves comfortably off and took a nice eighty-pound-a-year villa at Norbury. Our little place was very countrified, considering that it is so close to town. We had an inn and two houses a little above us, and a single cottage at the other side of the field which faces us, and except those there were no houses until you got halfway to the station. My business took me into town at certain seasons, but in summer I had less to do, and then in our country home my wife and I were just as happy as could be wished. I tell you that there never was a shadow between us until this accursed affair began.

'There's one thing I ought to tell you before I go further. When we married, my wife made over all her property to me—rather against my will, for I saw how awkward it would be if my business affairs went wrong. However, she would have it so, and it was done. Well, about six weeks ago she came to me.

'"Jack," said she, "when you took my money you said that if ever I wanted any I was to ask you for it."

'"Certainly" said I. "It's all your own."

'"Well," said she, "I want a hundred pounds."

'I was a bit staggered at this, for I had imagined it was simply a new dress or something of the kind that she was after.

'"What on earth for?" I asked.

'"Oh," said she in her playful way, "you said that you were only my banker, and bankers never ask questions, you know."

'"If you really mean it, of course you shall have the money," said I.

'"Oh, yes, I really mean it."

'"And you won't tell me what you want it for?"

'"Some day, perhaps, but not just at present, Jack."

'So I had to be content with that, though it was the first time that there had ever been any secret between us. I gave her a check, and I never thought any more of the matter. It may have nothing to do with what came afterwards, but I thought it only right to mention it.

'Well, I told you just now that there is a cottage not far from our house. There is just a field between us, but to reach it you have to go along the road and then turn down a lane. Just beyond it is a nice little grove of Scotch firs, and I used to be very fond of strolling down there, for trees are always a neighbourly kind of thing. The cottage had been standing empty this eight months, and it was a pity, for it was a pretty two-storied place, with an old-fashioned porch and a honeysuckle about it. I have stood many a time and thought what a neat little homestead it would make.

'Well, last Monday evening I was taking a stroll down that way when I met an empty van coming up the lane and saw a pile of carpets and things lying about on the grass-plot beside the porch. It was clear that the cottage had at last been let. I walked past it, and then stopping, as an idle man might, I ran my eye over it and wondered what sort of folk they were who had come to live so near us. And as I looked I suddenly became aware that a face was watching me out of one of the upper windows.

'I don't know what there was about that face, Mr Holmes, but it seemed to send a chill right down my back. I was some little way off, so that I could not make out the features, but there was something unnatural and inhuman about the face. That was the impression that I had, and I moved quickly forward to get a nearer view of the person who was watching me. But as I did so the face suddenly disappeared, so suddenly that it seemed to have been plucked away into the darkness of the room. I stood for five minutes thinking the business over and trying to analyze my impressions. I could not tell if the face was that of a man or a woman. It had been too far from me for that. But its colour was what had impressed me most. It was of a livid chalky white, and with something set and rigid about it which was shockingly unnatural. So disturbed was I that I determined to see a little more of the new inmates of the cottage. I approached and knocked at the door, which was instantly opened by a tall, gaunt woman with a harsh, forbidding face.

"'What may you be wantin'?" she asked in a Northern accent.

"I am your neighbour over yonder," said I, nodding towards my house. "I see that you have only just moved in, so I thought that if I could be of any help to you in any—"

"'Ay, we'll just ask ye when we want ye," said she, and shut the door in my face. Annoyed at the churlish rebuff, I turned my back and walked home. All evening, though I tried to think of other things, my mind would still turn to the apparition at the window and the rudeness of the woman. I determined to say nothing about the former to my wife, for she is a nervous, highly strung woman, and I had no wish that she should share the unpleasant impression which had been produced upon myself. I remarked to her, however, before I fell asleep, that the cottage was now occupied, to which she returned no reply.

'I am usually an extremely sound sleeper. It has been a standing jest in the family that nothing could ever wake me during the night. And yet somehow on that particular night, whether it may have been the slight excitement produced by my little adventure or not I know not, but I slept much more lightly than usual. Half in my dreams I was dimly conscious that something was going on in the room, and gradually became aware that my wife had dressed herself and was slipping on her mantle and her bonnet. My lips were parted to murmur out some sleepy words of surprise or remonstrance at this untimely preparation, when suddenly my half-opened eyes fell upon her face, illuminated by the candle-light, and astonishment held me dumb. She wore an expression such as I had never seen before—such as I should have thought her incapable of assuming. She was deadly pale and breathing fast, glancing furtively towards the bed as she fastened her mantle to see if she had disturbed me. Then thinking that I was still asleep, she slipped noiselessly from the room, and an instant later I heard a sharp creaking which could only come from the hinges of the front door. I sat up in bed and rapped my knuckles against the rail to make certain that I was truly awake. Then I took my watch from under the pillow. It was three in the morning. What on this earth could my wife be doing out on the country road at three in the morning?

'I had sat for about twenty minutes turning the thing over in my mind and trying to find some possible explanation. The more I thought, the more extraordinary and inexplicable did it appear. I was still puzzling over it when I heard the door gently close again, and her footsteps coming up the stairs.

'"Where in the world have you been, Effie?" I asked as she entered.

'She gave a violent start and a kind of gasping cry when I spoke, and that cry and start troubled me more than all the rest, for there was something indescribably guilty about them. My wife had always been a woman of a frank, open nature, and it gave me a chill to see her slinking into her own room and crying out and wincing when her own husband spoke to her.

'"You awake, Jack!" she cried with a nervous laugh. "Why, I thought that nothing could awake you."

'"Where have you been?" I asked, more sternly.

'"I don't wonder that you are surprised," said she, and I could see that her fingers were trembling as she undid the fastenings of her mantle. "Why, I never remember having done such a thing in my life before. The fact is that I felt as though I were choking and had a perfect longing for a breath of fresh air. I really think that I should have fainted if I had not gone out. I stood at the door for a few minutes, and now I am quite myself again."

'All the time that she was telling me this story she never once looked in my direction, and her voice was quite unlike her usual tones. It was evident to me that she was saying what was false. I said nothing in reply, but turned my face to the wall, sick at heart, with my mind filled with a thousand venomous doubts and suspicions. What was it that my wife was concealing from me? Where had she been during that strange expedition? I felt that I should have no peace until I knew, and yet I shrank from asking her again after once she had told me what was false. All the rest of the night I tossed and tumbled, framing theory after theory, each more unlikely than the last.

'I should have gone to the City that day, but I was too disturbed in my mind to be able to pay attention to business matters. My wife seemed to be as upset as myself, and I could see from the little questioning glances which she kept shooting at me that she understood that I disbelieved her statement, and that she was at her wit's end what to do. We hardly exchanged a word during breakfast, and immediately afterwards I went out for a walk that I might think the matter out in the fresh morning air.

'I went as far as the Crystal Palace, spent an hour in the grounds, and was back in Norbury by one o'clock. It happened that my way took me past the cottage, and I stopped for an instant to look at the windows and to see if I could catch a glimpse of the strange face which had looked out at me on the day before. As I stood there, imagine my surprise, Mr Holmes, when the door suddenly opened and my wife walked out.

'I was struck dumb with astonishment at the sight of her, but my emotions were nothing to those which showed themselves upon her face when our eyes met. She seemed for an instant to wish to shrink back inside the house again, and then, seeing how useless all concealment must be, she came forward, with a very white face and frightened eyes which belied the smile upon her lips.

'"Ah, Jack," she said, "I have just been in to see if I can be of any assistance to our new neighbours. Why do you look at me like that, Jack? You are not angry with me?"

'"So," said I, "this is where you went during the night."

'"What do you mean?" she cried.

'"You came here. I am sure of it. Who are these people that you should visit them at such an hour?"

'"I have not been here before."

'"How can you tell me what you know is false?" I cried. "Your very voice changes as you speak. When have I ever had a secret from you? I shall enter that cottage, and I shall probe the matter to the bottom."

'"No, no, Jack, for God's sake!" she gasped in uncontrollable emotion. Then, as I approached the door, she seized my sleeve and pulled me back with convulsive strength.

'"I implore you not to do this, Jack," she cried. "I swear that I will tell you everything some day, but nothing but misery can come of it if you enter that cottage." Then, as I tried to shake her off, she clung to me in a frenzy of entreaty.

'"Trust me, Jack!" she cried. "Trust me only this once. You will never have cause to regret it. You know that I would not have a secret from you if it were not for your own sake. Our whole lives are at stake in this. If you come home with me all will be well. If you force your way into that cottage all is over between us.'

'There was such earnestness, such despair, in her manner that her words arrested me, and I stood irresolute before the door.

'"I will trust you on one condition, and on one condition only," said I at last. "It is that this mystery comes to an end from now. You are at liberty to preserve your secret, but you must promise me that there shall be no more nightly visits, no more doings which are kept from my knowledge. I am willing to forget those which are past if you will promise that there shall be no more in the future."

'"I was sure that you would trust me," she cried with a great sigh of relief. "It shall be just as you wish. Come away—oh, come away up to the house."

'Still pulling at my sleeve, she led me away from the cottage. As we went I glanced back, and there was that yellow livid face watching us out of the upper window. What link could there be between that creature and my wife? Or how could the coarse, rough woman whom I had seen the day before be connected with her? It was a strange puzzle, and yet I knew that my mind could never know ease again until I had solved it.

'For two days after this I stayed at home, and my wife appeared to abide loyally by our engagement, for, as far as I know, she never stirred out of the house. On the third day however, I had ample evidence that her solemn promise was not enough to hold her back from this secret influence which drew her away from her husband and her duty.

'I had gone into town on that day, but I returned by the 2:40 instead of the 3:36, which is my usual train. As I entered the house the maid ran into the hall with a startled face.

'Where is your mistress?' I asked.

'I think that she has gone out for a walk,' she answered.

'My mind was instantly filled with suspicion. I rushed upstairs to make sure that she was not in the house. As I did so I happened to glance out of one of the upper windows and saw the maid with whom I had just been speaking running across the field in the direction of the cottage. Then of course I saw exactly what it all meant. My wife had gone over there and had asked the servant to call her if I should return. Tingling with anger, I rushed down and hurried across, determined to end the matter once and forever. I saw my wife and the maid hurrying back along the lane, but I did not stop to speak with them. In the cottage lay the secret which was casting a shadow over my life. I vowed that, come what might, it should be a secret no longer. I did not even knock when I reached it, but turned the handle and rushed into the passage.

'It was all still and quiet upon the ground floor. In the kitchen a kettle was singing on the fire, and a large black cat lay coiled up in the basket; but there was no sign of the woman whom I had seen before. I ran into the other room, but it was equally deserted. Then I rushed up the stairs only to find two other rooms empty and deserted at the top. There was no one at all in the whole house. The furniture and pictures were of the most common and vulgar description, save in the one chamber at the window of which I had seen the strange face. That was comfortable and elegant, and all my suspicions rose into a fierce, bitter flame when I saw that on the mantelpiece stood a copy of a full-length photograph of my wife, which had been taken at my request only three months ago.

'I stayed long enough to make certain that the house was absolutely empty. Then I left it, feeling a weight at my heart such as I had never had before. My wife came out into the hall as I entered my house; but I was too hurt and angry to speak with her, and, pushing past her, I made my way into my study. She followed me, however, before I could close the door.

'"I am sorry that I broke my promise, Jack," said she, "but if you knew all the circumstances I am sure that you would forgive me."

'"Tell me everything, then," said I.

'"I cannot, Jack, I cannot," she cried.

'"Until you tell me who it is that has been living in that cottage, and who it is to whom you have given that photograph, there can never be any confidence between us," said I, and breaking away from her I left the house. That was yesterday, Mr Holmes, and I have not seen her since, nor do I know anything more about this strange business. It is the first shadow that has come between us, and it has so shaken me that I do not know what I should do for the best. Suddenly this morning it occurred to me that you were the man to advise me, so I have hurried to you now, and I place myself unreservedly in your hands. If there is any point which I have not made clear, pray question me about it. But, above all, tell me quickly what I am to do. for this misery is more than I can bear.'

Holmes and I had listened with the utmost interest to this extraordinary statement, which had been delivered in the jerky, broken fashion of a man who is under the influence of extreme emotion. My companion sat silent now for some time, with his chin upon his hand, lost in thought.

'Tell me,' said he at last, 'could you swear that this was a man's face which you saw at the window?'

'Each time that I saw it I was some distance away from it so that is impossible for me to say.'

'You appear, however, to have been disagreeably impressed by it.'

'It seemed to be of an unusual colour and to have a strange rigidity about the features. When I approached it vanished with a jerk.'

'How long is it since your wife asked you for a hundred pounds?'

'Nearly two months.'

'Have you ever seen a photograph of her first husband?'

'No, there was a great fire at Atlanta very shortly after his death, and all her papers were destroyed.'

'And yet she had a certificate of death. You say that you saw it.'

'Yes, she got a duplicate after the fire.'

'Did you ever meet anyone who knew her in America?'

'No.'

'Did she ever talk of revisiting the place?'

'No.'

'Or get letters from it?'

'No.'

'Thank you. I should like to think over the matter a little now. If the cottage is now permanently deserted we may have some difficulty. If, on the other hand, as I fancy is more likely the inmates were warned of your coming and left before you entered yesterday, then they may be back now, and we should clear it all up easily. Let me advise you, then, to return to Norbury and to examine the windows of the cottage again. If you have reason to believe that it is inhabited, do not force your way in, but send a wire to my friend and me. We shall be with you within an hour of receiving it, and we shall then very soon get to the bottom of the business.'

'And if it is still empty?'

'In that case I shall come out tomorrow and talk it over with you. Good-bye, and, above all, do not fret until you know that you really have a cause for it.'

'I am afraid that this is a bad business, Watson,' said my companion as he returned after accompanying Mr Grant Munro to the door. 'What do you make of it?'

'It had an ugly sound,' I answered.

'Yes. There's blackmail in it, or I am much mistaken.'

'And who is the blackmailer?'

'Well, it must be the creature who lives in the only comfortable room in the place and has her photograph above his fireplace. Upon my word, Watson, there is something very attractive about that livid face at the window, and I would not have missed the case for worlds.'

'You have a theory?'

'Yes, a provisional one. But I shall be surprised if it does not turn out to be correct. This woman's first husband is in that cottage.'

'Why do you think so?'

'How else can we explain her frenzied anxiety that her second one should not enter it? The facts, as I read them, are something like this: This woman was married in America. Her husband developed some hateful qualities, or shall we say he contracted some loathsome disease and became a leper or an imbecile? She flies from him at last, returns to England, changes her name, and starts her life, as she thinks, afresh. She has been married three years and believes that her position is quite secure, having shown her husband the death certificate of some man whose name she has assumed, when suddenly her whereabouts is discovered by her first husband, or, we may suppose, by some unscrupulous woman who has attached herself to the invalid. They write to the wife and threaten to come and expose her. She asks for a hundred pounds and endeavours to buy them off. They come in spite of it, and when the husband mentions casually to the wife that there are newcomers in the cottage, she knows in some way that they are her pursuers. She waits until her husband is asleep and then she rushes down to endeavour to persuade them to leave her in peace. Having no success, she goes again next morning, and her husband meets her, as he has told us, as she comes out. She promises him then not to go there again, but two days afterwards, the hope of getting rid of those dreadful neighbours was too strong for her, and she made another attempt, taking down with her the photograph which had probably been demanded from her. In the midst of this interview the maid rushed in to say that the master had come home, on which the wife, knowing that he would come straight down to the cottage, hurried the inmates out at the back door, into the grove of fir-trees, probably, which was mentioned as standing near. In this way he found the place deserted. I shall be very much surprised, however, if it is still so when he reconnoitres it this evening. What do you think of my theory?'

'It is all surmise.'

'But at least it covers all the facts. When new facts come to our knowledge which cannot be covered by it, it will be time enough to reconsider it. We can do nothing more until we have a message from our friend at Norbury.'

But we had not a very long time to wait for that. It came just as we had finished our tea.

'The cottage is still tenanted', it said. 'Have seen the face again at the window. Will meet the seven o'clock train and will take no steps until you arrive.'

He was waiting on the platform when we stepped out, and we could see in the light of the station lamps that he was very pale, and quivering with agitation.

'They are still there, Mr Holmes,' said he, laying his hand hard upon my friend's sleeve. 'I saw lights in the cottage as I came down. We shall settle it now once and for all.'

'What is your plan, then?' asked Holmes as he walked down the dark tree-lined road.

'I am going to force my way in and see for myself who is in the house. I wish you both to be there as witnesses.'

'You are quite determined to do this in spite of your wife's warning that it is better that you should not solve the mystery?'

'Yes, I am deterrnined.'

'Well, I think that you are in the right. Any truth is better than indefinite doubt. We had better go up at once. Of course, legally, we are putting ourselves hopelessly in the wrong; but I think that it is worth it.'

It was a very dark night, and a thin rain began to fall as

we turned from the highroad into a narrow lane, deeply rutted, with hedges on either side. Mr Grant Munro pushed impatiently forward, however, and we stumbled after him as best we could.

'There are the lights of my house,' he murmured, pointing to a glimmer among the trees. 'And here is the cottage which I am going to enter.'

We turned a corner in the lane as he spoke, and there was the building close beside us. A yellow bar falling across the black foreground showed that the door was not quite closed, and one window in the upper story was brightly illuminated. As we looked, we saw a dark blur moving across the blind.

'There is that creature!' cried Grant Munro. 'You can see for yourselves that someone is there. Now follow me, and we shall soon know all.'

We approached the door, but suddenly a woman appeared out of the shadow and stood in the golden track of the lamplight. I could not see her face in the darkness, but her arms were thrown out in an attitude of entreaty.

'For God's sake, don't, Jack!' she cried. 'I had a presentiment that you would come this evening. Think better of it, dear! Trust me again, and you will never have cause to regret it.'

'I have trusted you too long, Effie,' he cried sternly. 'Leave go of me! I must pass you. My friends and I are going to settle this matter once and forever!' He pushed her to one side, and we followed closely after him. As he threw the door open an old woman ran out in front of him and tried to bar his passage, but he thrust her back, and an instant afterwards we were all upon the stairs. Grant Munro rushed into the lighted room at the top, and we entered at his heels.

It was a cosy, well-furnished apartment, with two candles burning upon the table and two upon the mantelpiece. In the corner, stooping over a desk, there sat what appeared to be a little girl. Her face was turned away as we entered, but we could see that she was dressed in a red frock, and that she had long white gloves on. As she whisked round to us, I gave a cry of surprise and horror. The face which she turned towards us was of the strangest livid tint, and the features were absolutely devoid of any expression. An instant later the mystery was explained. Holmes, with a laugh, passed his hand behind the child's ear, a mask peeled off from her countenance, and there was a little coal-black negress, with all her white teeth flashing in amusement at our amazed faces. I burst out laughing, out of sympathy with her merriment; but Grant Munro stood staring, with his hand clutching his throat.

'My God!' he cried. 'What can be the meaning of this?'

'I will tell you the meaning of it,' cried the lady, sweeping into the room with a proud, set face. 'You have forced me, against my own judgment, to tell you, and now we must both make the best of it. My husband died at Atlanta. My child survived.'

'Your child?'

She drew a large silver locket from her bosom. 'You have never seen this open.'

'I understood that it did not open.'

She touched a spring, and the front hinged back. There was a portrait within of a man strikingly handsome and intelligent-looking, but bearing unmistakable signs upon his features of his African descent.

'That is John Hebron, of Atlanta,' said the lady, 'and a nobler man never walked the earth. I cut myself off from my race in order to wed him, but never once while he lived did I for an instant regret it. It was our misfortune that our only child took after his people rather than mine. It is often so in such matches, and little Lucy is darker far than ever her father was. But dark or fair, she is my own dear little girlie, and her mother's pet.' The little creature ran across at the words and nestled up against the lady's dress. 'When I left her in America,' she continued, 'it was only because her health was weak, and the change might have done her harm. She was given to the care of a faithful Scotch woman who had once been our servant. Never for an instant did I dream of disowning her as my child. But when chance threw you in my way, Jack, and I learned to love you, I feared to tell you about my child. God forgive me, I feared that I should lose you, and I had not the courage to tell you. I had to choose between you, and in my weakness I turned away from my own little girl. For three years I have kept her existence a secret from you, but I heard from the nurse, and I knew that all was well with her. At last, however, there came an overwhelming desire to see the child once more. I struggled against it, but in vain. Though I knew the danger, I determined to have the child over, if it were but for a few weeks. I sent a hundred pounds to the nurse, and I gave her instructions about this cottage, so that she might come as a neighbour, without my appearing to be in any way connected with her. I pushed my precautions so far as to order her to keep the child in the house during the daytime, and to cover up her little face and hands so that even those who might see her at the window should not gossip about there being a black child in the neighbourhood. If I had been less cautious I might have been more wise. but I was half crazy with fear that you should learn the truth.

It was you who told me first that the cottage was occupied. I should have waited for the morning, but I could not sleep for excitement, and so at last I slipped out, knowing how difficult it is to awake you. But you saw me go, and that was the beginning of my troubles. Next day you had my secret at your mercy, but you nobly refrained from pursuing your advantage. Three days later, however, the nurse and child only just escaped from the back door as you rushed in at the front one. And now tonight you at last know all, and I ask you what is to become of us, my child and me?' She clasped her hands and waited for an answer.

It was a long ten minutes before Grant Munro broke the silence, and when his answer came it was one of which I love to think. He lifted the little child, kissed her, and then, still carrying her, he held his other hand out to his wife and turned towards the door.

'We can talk it over more comfortably at home,' said he. 'I am not a very good man, Effie, but I think that I am a better one than you have given me credit for being.'

Holmes and I followed them down the lane, and my friend plucked at my sleeve as we came out.

'I think,' said he, 'that we shall be of more use in London than in Norbury.'

Not another word did he say of the case until late that night, when he was turning away, with his lighted candle, for his bedroom.

'Watson,' said he, 'if it should ever strike you that I am getting a little overconfident in my powers, or giving less pains to a case than it deserves, kindly whisper "Norbury" in my ear, and I shall be infinitely obliged to you.'

5

THE ADVENTURE OF THE STOCKBROKER'S CLERK

Shortly after my marriage I had bought a connection in the Paddington district. Old Mr Farquhar, from whom I purchased it, had at one time an excellent general practice; but his age, and an affliction of the nature of St. Vitus's dance from which he suffered, had very much thinned it. The public not unnaturally goes on the principle that he who would heal others must himself be whole, and looks askance at the curative powers of the man whose own case is beyond the reach of his drugs. Thus as my predecessor weakened his practice declined, until when I purchased it from him it had sunk from twelve hundred to little more than three hundred a year. I had confidence, however, in my own youth and energy and was convinced that in a very few years the concern would be as flourishing as ever.

For three months after taking over the practice I was kept very closely at work and saw little of my friend Sherlock Holmes, for I was too busy to visit Baker Street, and he seldom went anywhere himself save upon professional business. I was surprised, therefore, when, one morning in June, as I sat reading the British Medical Journal after breakfast, I heard a ring at the bell, followed by the high, somewhat strident tones of my old companion's voice.

'Ah, my dear Watson,' said he, striding into the room, 'I am very delighted to see you! I trust that Mrs Watson has entirely recovered from all the little excitements connected with our adventure of the Sign of Four.'

'Thank you, we are both very well,' said I, shaking him warmly by the hand.

'And I hope, also,' he continued, sitting down in the rockingchair, 'that the cares of medical practice have not entirely obliterated the interest which you used to take in our little deductive problems.'

'On the contrary,' I answered, 'it was only last night that I was looking over my old notes, and classifying some of our past results.'

'I trust that you don't consider your collection closed.'

'Not at all. I should wish nothing better than to have some more of such experiences.'

'Today, for example?'

'Yes, today, if you like.'

'And as far off as Birmingham?'

'Certainly, if you wish it.'

'And the practice?'

'I do my neighbour's when he goes. He is always ready to work off the debt.'

'Ha! nothing could be better,' said Holmes, leaning back in his chair and looking keenly at me from under his half-closed lids. 'I perceive that you have been unwell lately. Summer colds are always a little trying.'

'I was confined to the house by a severe chill for three days last week. I thought, however, that I had cast off every trace of it.'

'So you have. You look remarkably robust.'

'How, then, did you know of it?'

'My dear fellow, you know my methods.'

'You deduced it, then?'

'Certainly.'

'And from what?'

'From your slippers.'

I glanced down at the new patent-leathers which I was wearing. 'How on earth—' I began, but Holmes answered my question before it was asked.

'Your slippers are new,' he said. 'You could not have had them more than a few weeks. The soles which you are at this moment presenting to me are slightly scorched. For a moment I thought they might have got wet and been burned in the drying. But near the instep there is a small circular wafer of paper with the shopman's hieroglyphics upon it. Damp would of course have removed this. You had, then, been sitting with your feet outstretched to the fire, which a man would hardly do even in so wet a June as this if he were in his full health.'

Like all Holmes's reasoning the thing seemed simplicity itself when it was once explained. He read the thought upon my features, and his smile had a tinge of bitterness.

'I am afraid that I rather give myself away when I explain.' said he. 'Results without causes are much more impressive. You are ready to come to Birmingham. then?'

'Certainly. What is the case?'

'You shall hear it all in the train. My client is outside in a four-wheeler. Can you come at once?'

'In an instant.' I scribbled a note to my neighbour, rushed upstairs to explain the matter to my wife, and joined Holmes upon the doorstep.

'Your neighbour is a doctor.' said he, nodding at the brass plate.

'Yes, he bought a practice as I did.'

'An old-established one?'

'Just the same as mine. Both have been ever since the houses were built.'

'Ah! then you got hold of the best of the two.'

'I think I did. But how do you know?'

'By the steps, my boy. Yours are worn three inches deeper than his. But this gentleman in the cab is my client, Mr Hall Pycroft. Allow me to introduce you to him. Whip your horse up, cabby, for we have only just time to catch our train.'

The man whom I found myself facing was a well-built, fresh-complexioned young fellow, with a frank, honest face and a slight, crisp, yellow moustache. He wore a very shiny top-hat and a neat suit of sober black, which made him look what he was—a smart young City man, of the class who have been labelled cockneys, but who give us our crack volunteer regiments, and who turn out more fine athletes and sportsmen than anybody of men in these islands. His round, ruddy face was naturally full of cheeriness, but the corners of his mouth seemed to me to be pulled down in a half-comical distress. It was not, however, until we were in a first-class carriage and well started upon our journey to Birmingham that I was able to learn what the trouble was which had driven him to Sherlock Holmes.

'We have a clear run here of seventy minutes,' Holmes remarked. 'I want you, Mr Hall Pycroft, to tell my friend your very interesting experience exactly as you have told it to me, or with more detail if possible. It will be of use to me to hear the succession of events again. It is a case, Watson, which may prove to have something in it, or may prove to have nothing, but which, at least, presents those unusual and outre features which are as dear to you as they are to me. Now, Mr Pycroft. I shall not interrupt you again.'

Our young companion looked at me with a twinkle in his eye.

'The worst of the story is.' said he. 'that I show myself up as such a confounded fool. Of course it may work out all right. and I don't see that I could have done otherwise; but if I have lost my crib and get nothing in exchange I shall feel what a soft Johnnie I have been. I'm not very good at telling a story, Dr. Watson, but it is like this with me:

'I used to have a billet at Coxon & Woodhouse's, of Draper Gardens, but they were let in early in the spring through the Venezuelan loan, as no doubt you remember, and came a nasty cropper. I have been with them five years. and old Coxon gave me a ripping good testimonial when the smash came. but of course we clerks were all turned adrift, the twenty-seven of us. I tried here and tried there, but there were lots of other chaps on the same lay as myself, and it was a perfect frost for a long time. I had been taking three pounds a week at Coxon's, and I had saved about seventy of them, but I soon worked my way through that and out at the other end. I was fairly at the end of my tether at last, and could hardly find the stamps to answer the advertisements or the envelopes to stick them to. I had worn out my boots paddling up office stairs, and I seemed just as far from getting a billet as ever.

'At last I saw a vacancy at Mawson & Williams's, the great stock-broking firm in Lombard Street. I dare say E. C. is not much in your line, but I can tell you that this is about the richest house in London. The advertisement was to be answered by letter only. I sent in my testimonial and application, but without the least hope of getting it. Back came an answer by return, saying that if I would appear next Monday I might take over my new duties at once, provided that my appearance was satisfactory. No one knows how these things are worked. Some people say that the manager just plunges his hand into the heap and takes the first that comes. Anyhow it was my innings that time, and I don't ever wish to feel better pleased. The screw was a pound a week rise, and the duties just about the same as at Coxon's.

'And now I come to the queer part of the business. I was in diggings out Hampstead way, 17 Potter's Terrace. Well, I was sitting doing a smoke that very evening after I had been promised the appointment, when up came my landlady with a card which had "Arthur Pinner, Financial Agent," printed upon it. I had never heard the name before and could not imagine what he wanted with me, but of course I asked her to show him up. In he walked, a middle-sized dark-haired, dark-eyed, black-bearded man, with a touch of the sheeny about his nose. He had a brisk kind of way with him and spoke sharply, like a man who knew the value of time.

"'Mr Hall Pycroft, I believe?' said he.

"'Yes, sir,' I answered, pushing a chair towards him.

"'Lately engaged at Coxon & Woodhouse's?'

"'Yes, sir.'

"'And now on the staff of Mawson's.'

"'Quite so.'

"'Well,' said he, 'the fact is that I have heard some really extraordinary stories about your financial ability. You remember Parker, who used to be Coxon's manager. He can never say enough about it.'

'Of course I was pleased to hear this. I had always been pretty sharp in the office, but I had never dreamed that I was talked about in the City in this fashion.

"'You have a good memory?' said he.

"'Pretty fair,' I answered modestly.

"'Have you kept in touch with the market while you have been out of work?' he asked.

"'Yes. I read the stock-exchange list every morning.'

"'Now that shows real application!' he cried. 'That is the way to prosper! You won't mind my testing you, will you? Let me see. How are Ayrshires?'

"'A hundred and six and a quarter to a hundred and five and seven-eighths.'

"'And New Zealand consolidated?'

"'A hundred and four.'

"'And British Broken Hills?'

"'Seven to seven-and-six.'

"'Wonderful!' he cried with his hands up. 'This quite fits in with all that I had heard. My boy, my boy, you are very much too good to be a clerk at Mawson's!"

'This outburst rather astonished me, as you can think. "Well," said I, "other people don't think quite so much of me as you seem to do, Mr Pinner. I had a hard enough fight to get this berth, and I am very glad to have it."

"'Pooh, man; you should soar above it. You are not in your true sphere. Now, I'll tell you how it stands with me. What I have to offer is little enough when measured by your ability, but when compared with Mawson's it's light to dark. Let me see. When do you go to Mawson's?"

"'On Monday.'

"'Ha, ha! I think I would risk a little sporting flutter that you don't go there at all."

"'Not go to Mawson's?"

"'No, sir. By that day you will be the business manager of the Franco-Midland Hardware Company, Limited, with a hundred and thirty-four branches in the towns and villages of France, not counting one in Brussels and one in San Remo."

"'This took my breath away. "'I never heard of it." said I.

"'Very likely not. It has been kept very quiet, for the capital was all privately subscribed, and it's too good a thing to let the public into. My brother, Harry Pinner, is promoter, and joins the board after allotment as managing director. He knew I was in the swim down here and asked me to pick up a good man cheap. A young, pushing man with plenty of snap about him. Parker spoke of you, and that brought me here tonight. We can only offer you a beggarly five hundred to start with."

"'Five hundred a year!" I shouted.

"'Only that at the beginning; but you are to have an overriding commission of one per cent on all business done by your agents, and you may take my word for it that this will come to more than your salary."

'"But I know nothing about hardware."

'"Tut, my boy, you know about figures."

'My head buzzed, and I could hardly sit still in my chair. But suddenly a little chill of doubt came upon me.

'"I must be frank with you," said I. "Mawson only gives me two hundred, but Mawson is safe. Now, really, I know so little about your company that—"

'"Ah, smart, smart!" he cried in a kind of ecstasy of delight. "You are the very man for us. You are not to be talked over, and quite right, too. Now, here's a note for a hundred pounds, and if you think that we can do business you may just slip it into your pocket as an advance upon your salary."

'"That is very handsome," said I. "When should I take over my new duties?"

'"Be in Birmingham tomorrow at one," said he. "I have a note in my pocket here which you will take to my brother. You will find him at 126B Corporation Street. where the temporary offices of the company are situated. Of course he must confirm your engagement, but between ourselves it will be all right."

'"Really, I hardly know how to express my gratitude, Mr Pinner," said I.

'"Not at all, my boy. You have only got your deserts. There are one or two small things—mere formalities—which I must arrange with you. You have a bit of paper beside you there. Kindly write upon it 'I am perfectly willing to act as business manager to the Franco-Midland Hardware Company, Limited, at a minimum salary of £500.'

'I did as he asked. and he put the paper in his pocket.

'"There is one other detail," said he. "What do you intend to do about Mawson's?"

'I had forgotten all about Mawson's in my joy. "I'll write and resign," said I.

'"Precisely what I don't want you to do. I had a row over you with Mawson's manager. I had gone up to ask him about you, and he was very offensive; accused me of coaxing you away from the service of the firm, and that sort of thing. At last I fairly lost my temper. "If you want good men you should pay them a good price," said I.

'He would rather have our small price than your big one,' said he.

'I'll lay you a fiver,' said I, 'that when he has my offer you'll never so much as hear from him again.'

'Done!' said he. 'We picked him out of the gutter, and he won't leave us so easily.' Those were his very words.'

'"The impudent scoundrel!" I cried. "I've never so much as seen him in my life. Why should I consider him in any way? I shall certainly not write if you would rather I didn't."

'"Good! That's a promise," said he, rising from his chair. "Well, I'm delighted to have got so good a man for my brother. Here's your advance of a hundred pounds, and here is the letter. Make a note of the address. 126B Corporation Street, and remember that one o'clock tomorrow is your appointment. Good-night, and may you have all the fortune that you deserve!"

'That's just about all that passed between us, as near as I can remember. You can imagine, Dr. Watson, how pleased I was at such an extraordinary bit of good fortune. I sat up half the night hugging myself over it, and next day I was off to Birmingham in a train that would take me in plenty time for my appointment. I took my things to a hotel in New Street, and then I made my way to the address which had been given me.

'It was a quarter of an hour before my time, but I thought that would make no difference. 126B was a passage between two large shops, which led to a winding stone stair, from which there were many flats, let as offices to companies or professional men. The names of the occupants were painted at the bottom on the wall, but there was no such name as the Franco-Midland Hardware

Company, Limited. I stood for a few minutes with my heart in my boots, wondering whether the whole thing was an elaborate hoax or not, when up came a man and addressed me. He was very like the chap I had seen the night before, the same figure and voice, but he was clean-shaven and his hair was lighter.

"Are you Mr Hall Pycroft?" he asked.

"Yes," said I.

"Oh! I was expecting you, but you are a trifle before your time. I had a note from my brother this morning in which he sang your praises very loudly."

"I was just looking for the offices when you came."

"We have not got our name up yet, for we only secured these temporary premises last week. Come up with me, and we will talk the matter over."

'I followed him to the top of a very lofty stair, and there, right under the slates, were a couple of empty, dusty little rooms, uncarpeted and uncurtained, into which he led me. I had thought of a great office with shining tables and rows of clerks, such as I was used to, and I daresay I stared rather straight at the two deal chairs and one little table, which with a ledger and a waste-paper basket, made up the whole furniture.

"Don't be disheartened, Mr Pycroft," said my new acquaintance, seeing the length of my face. "Rome was not built in a day, and we have lots of money at our backs, though we don't cut much dash yet in offices. Pray sit down, and let me have your letter."

'I gave it to him, and he read it over very carefully.

"'You seem to have made a vast impression upon my brother Arthur," said he, "and I know that he is a pretty shrewd judge. He swears by London, you know; and I by Birmingham; but this time I shall follow his advice. Pray consider yourself definitely engaged."

"'What are my duties?" I asked.

"'You will eventually manage the great depot in Paris, which will pour a flood of English crockery into the shops of a hundred and thirty-four agents in France. The purchase will be completed in a week, and meanwhile you will remain in Birmingham and make yourself useful."

"'How?'"

'For answer, he took a big red book out of a drawer.

"'This is a directory of Paris,' said he, "with the trades after the names of the people. I want you to take it home with you and to mark off all the hardware-sellers, with their addresses. It would be of the greatest use to me to have them."

"'Surely, there are classified lists?" I suggested.

"'Not reliable ones. Their system is different from ours. Stick at it, and let me have the lists by Monday, at twelve. Good-day, Mr Pycroft. If you continue to show zeal and intelligence you will find the company a good master."

'I went back to the hotel with the big book under my arm, and with very conflicting feelings in my breast. On the one hand, I was definitely engaged and had a hundred pounds in my pocket; on the other, the look of the offices, the absence of name on the wall, and other of the points which would strike a business man had left a bad impression as to the position of my employers. However, come what might, I had my money, so l settled down to my task. All Sunday I was kept hard at work, and yet by Monday I had only got as far as H. I went round to my employer, found him in the same dismantled kind of room, and was told to keep at it until Wednesday, and then come again. On Wednesday it was still unfinished, so I hammered away until Friday—that is, yesterday. Then I brought it round to Mr Harry Pinner.

"'Thank you very much," said he, "I fear that I underrated the difficulty of the task. This list will be of very material assistance to me."

"It took some time," said I.

"'And now," said he, "I want you to make a list of the furniture shops, for they all sell crockery."

'"Very good."

'"And you can come up tomorrow evening at seven and let me know how you are getting on. Don't overwork yourself. A couple of hours at Day's Music Hall in the evening would do you no harm after your labours." He laughed as he spoke, and I saw with a thrill that his second tooth upon the left-hand side had been very badly stuffed with gold.'

Sherlock Holmes rubbed his hands with delight, and I stared with astonishment at our client.

'You may well look surprised, Dr. Watson, but it is this way,' said he: 'When I was speaking to the other chap in London, at the time that he laughed at my not going to Mawson's, I happened to notice that his tooth was stuffed in this very identical fashion. The glint of the gold in each case caught my eye, you see. When I put that with the voice and figure being the same, and only those things altered which might be changed by a razor or a wig, I could not doubt that it was the same man. Of course you expect two brothers to be alike, but not that they should have the same tooth stuffed in the same way. He bowed me out, and I found myself in the street, hardly knowing whether I was on my head or my heels. Back I went to my hotel, put my head in a basin of cold water, and tried to think it out. Why had he sent me from London to Birmingham? Why had he got there before me? And why had he written a letter from himself to himself? It was altogether too much for me, and I could make no sense of it. And then suddenly it struck me that what was dark to me might be very light to Mr Sherlock Holmes. I had just time to get up to town by the night train to see him this morning, and to bring you both back with me to Birmingham.'

There was a pause after the stock-broker's clerk had concluded his surprising experience. Then Sherlock Holmes cocked his eye at me, leaning back on the cushions with a pleased and yet critical face, like a connoisseur who has just taken his first sip of a comet vintage.

'Rather fine, Watson, is it not?' said he. 'There are points in it which please me. I think that you will agree with me that an interview with Mr Arthur Harry Pinner in the temporary offices of the Franco-Midland Hardware Company, Limited, would be a rather interesting experience for both of us.'

'But how can we do it?' I asked.

'Oh, easily enough,' said Hall Pycroft cheerily. 'You are two friends of mine who are in want of a billet, and what could be more natural than that I should bring you both round to the managing director?'

'Quite so, of course,' said Holmes. 'I should like to have a look at the gentleman and see if I can make anything of his little game. What qualities have you, my friend, which would make your services so valuable? Or is it possible that—' He began biting his nails and staring blankly out of the window, and we hardly drew another word from him until we were in New Street.

At seven o'clock that evening we were walking, the three of us, down Corporation Street to the company's offices.

'It is no use our being at all before our time,' said our client. 'He only comes there to see me, apparently, for the place is deserted up to the very hour he names.'

'That is suggestive,' remarked Holmes.

'By Jove, I told you so!' cried the clerk. 'That's he walking ahead of us there.'

He pointed to a smallish, dark, well-dressed man who was bustling along the other side of the road. As we watched him he looked across at a boy who was bawling out the latest edition of the evening paper, and, running over among the cabs and busses, he bought one from him. Then, clutching it in his hand, he vanished through a doorway.

'There he goes!' cried Hall Pycroft. 'These are the company's offices into which he has gone. Come with me, and I'll fix it up as easily as possible.'

Following his lead, we ascended five stories, until we found ourselves outside a half-opened door, at which our client tapped. A voice within bade us enter, and we entered a bare, unfurnished room such as Hall Pycroft had described. At the single table sat the man whom we had seen in the street, with his evening paper spread out in front of him, and as he looked up at us it seemed to me that I had never looked upon a face which bore such marks of grief, and of something beyond grief—of a horror such as comes to few men in a lifetime. His brow glistened with perspiration, his cheeks were of the dull, dead white of a fish's belly, and his eyes were wild and staring. He looked at his clerk as though he failed to recognize him, and I could see by the astonishment depicted upon our conductor's face that this was by no means the usual appearance of his employer.

'You look ill, Mr Pinner!' he exclaimed.

'Yes, I am not very well,' answered the other, making obvious efforts to pull himself together and licking his dry lips before he spoke. 'Who are these gentlemen whom you have brought with you?'

'One is Mr Harris, of Bermondsey, and the other is Mr Price, of this town,' said our clerk glibly. 'They are friends of mine and gentlemen of experience, but they have been out of a place for some little time, and they hoped that perhaps you might find an opening for them in the company's employment.'

'Very possibly! Very possibly!' cried Mr Pinner with a ghastly smile. 'Yes, I have no doubt that we shall be able to do something for you. What is your particular line, Mr Harris?'

'I am an accountant,' said Holmes.

'Ah, yes, we shall want something of the sort. And you. Mr Price?'

'A clerk,' said I.

'I have every hope that the company may accommodate you. I will let you know about it as soon as we come to any conclusion. And now I beg that you will go. For God's sake leave me to myself!'

These last words were shot out of him, as though the constraint which he was evidently setting upon himself had suddenly and utterly burst asunder. Holmes and I glanced at each other, and Hall Pycroft took a step towards the table.

'You forget, Mr Pinner, that I am here by appointment to receive some directions from you,' said he.

'Certainly, Mr Pycroft, certainly,' the other resumed in a calmer tone. 'You may wait here a moment and there is no reason why your friends should not wait with you. I will be entirely at your service in three minutes, if I might trespass upon your patience so far.' He rose with a very courteous air, and, bowing to us, he passed out through a door at the farther end of the room, which he closed behind him.

'What now?' whispered Holmes. 'Is he giving us the slip?'

'Impossible,' answered Pycroft.

'Why so?'

'That door leads into an inner room.'

'There is no exit?'

'None.'

'Is it furnished?'

'It was empty yesterday.'

'Then what on earth can he be doing? There is something which I don't understand in this matter. If ever a man was three parts mad with terror, that man's name is Pinner. What can have put the shivers on him?'

'He suspects that we are detectives,' I suggested.

'That's it,' cried Pycroft.

Holmes shook his head. 'He did not turn pale. He was pale when we entered the room,' said he. 'It is just possible that—'

His words were interrupted by a sharp rat-tat from the direction of the inner door.

'What the deuce is he knocking at his own door for?' cried the clerk.

Again and much louder came the rat-tat-tat. We all gazed expectantly at the closed door. Glancing at Holmes, I saw his face turn rigid, and he leaned forward in intense excitement. Then suddenly came a low guggling, gargling sound, and a brisk drumming upon woodwork. Holmes sprang frantically across the room and pushed at the door. It was fastened on the inner side. Following his example, we threw ourselves upon it with all our weight. One hinge snapped, then the other, and down came the door with a crash. Rushing over it, we found ourselves in the inner room. It was empty.

But it was only for a moment that we were at fault. At one corner, the corner nearest the room which we had left, there was a second door. Holmes sprang to it and pulled it open. A coat and waistcoat were lying on the floor, and from a hook behind the door, with his own braces round his neck, was hanging the managing director of the Franco-Midland Hardware Company. His knees were drawn up, his head hung at a dreadful angle to his body, and the clatter of his heels against the door made the noise which had broken in upon our conversation. In an instant I had caught him round the waist, and held him up while Holmes and Pycroft untied the elastic bands which had disappeared between the livid creases of skin. Then we carried him into the other room, where he lay with a clay-coloured face, puffing his purple lips in and out with every breath—a dreadful wreck of all that he had been but five minutes before.

'What do you think of him, Watson?' asked Holmes.

I stooped over him and examined him. His pulse was feeble and intermittent, but his breathing grew longer, and there was a little shivering of his eyelids, which showed a thin white slit of ball beneath.

'It has been touch and go with him,' said I, 'but he'll live now. Just open that window, and hand me the water carafe.' I undid his collar, poured the cold water over his face, and raised and sank his arms until he drew a long, natural breath. 'It's only a question of time now,' said I, as I turned away from him.

Holmes stood by the table, with his hands deep in his trousers' pockets and his chin upon his breast.

'I suppose we ought to call the police in now,' said he. 'And yet I confess that I'd like to give them a complete case when they come.'

'It's a blessed mystery to me,' cried Pycroft, scratching his head. 'Whatever they wanted to bring me all the way up here for, and then—'

'Pooh! All that is clear enough,' said Holmes impatiently. 'It is this last sudden move.'

'You understand the rest, then?'

'I think that it is fairly obvious. What do you say, Watson?'

I shrugged my shoulders. 'I must confess that I am out of my depths,' said I.

'Oh, surely if you consider the events at first they can only point to one conclusion.'

'What do you make of them?'

'Well, the whole thing hinges upon two points. The first is the making of Pycroft write a declaration by which he entered the service of this preposterous company. Do you not see how very suggestive that is?'

'I am afraid I miss the point.'

'Well, why did they want him to do it? Not as a business matter, for these arrangements are usually verbal, and there was no earthly business reason why this should be an exception. Don't you see, my young friend, that they were very anxious to obtain a specimen of your handwriting, and had no other way of doing it?'

'And why?'

'Quite so. Why? When we answer that we have made some progress with our little problem. Why? There can be only one adequate reason. Someone wanted to learn to imitate your writing and had to procure a specimen of it first. And now if we pass on to the second point we find that each throws light upon the other. That point is the request made by Pinner that you should not resign your place, but should leave the manager of this important business in the full expectation that a Mr Hall Pycroft, whom he had never seen, was about to enter the office upon the Monday morning.'

'My God!' cried our client, 'what a blind beetle I have been!'

'Now you see the point about the handwriting. Suppose that someone turned up in your place who wrote a completely different hand from that in which you had applied for the vacancy, of course the game would have been up. But in the interval the rogue had learned to imitate you, and his position was therefore secure, as I presume that nobody in the office had ever set eyes upon you.'

'Not a soul,' groaned Hall Pycroft.

'Very good. Of course it was of the utmost importance to prevent you from thinking better of it, and also to keep you from coming into contact with anyone who might tell you that your double was at work in Mawson's office. Therefore they gave you a handsome advance on your salary, and ran you off to the Midlands, where they gave you enough work to do to prevent your going to London, where you might have burst their little game up. That is all plain enough.'

'But why should this man pretend to be his own brother?'

'Well, that is pretty clear also. There are evidently only two of them in it. The other is impersonating you at the office. This one acted as your engager, and then found that he could not find you an employer without admitting a third person into his plot. That he was most unwilling to do. He changed his appearance as far as he could, and trusted that the likeness, which you could not fail to observe, would be put down to a family resemblance. But for the happy chance of the gold stuffing, your suspicions would probably never have been aroused.'

Hall Pycroft shook his clenched hands in the air. 'Good Lord!' he cried, 'while I have been fooled in this way, what has this other Hall Pycroft been doing at Mawson's? What should we do, Mr Holmes? Tell me what to do.'

'We must wire to Mawson's.'

'They shut at twelve on Saturdays.'

'Never mind. There may be some door-keeper or attendant—'

'Ah, yes, they keep a permanent guard there on account of the value of the securities that they hold. I remember hearing it talked of in the City.'

'Very good, we shall wire to him and see if all is well, and if a clerk of your name is working there. That is clear enough, but what is not so clear is why at sight of us one of the rogues should instantly walk out of the room and hang himself.'

'The paper!' croaked a voice behind us. The man was sitting up, blanched and ghastly, with returning reason in his eyes, and hands which rubbed nervously at the broad red band which still encircled his throat.

'The paper! Of course!' yelled Holmes in a paroxysm of excitement. 'Idiot that I was! I thought so much of our visit that the paper never entered my head for an instant. To be sure, the secret must lie there.' He flattened it out upon the table, and a cry of triumph burst from his lips. 'Look at this, Watson,' he cried. 'It is a London paper, an early edition of the Evening Standard. Here is what we want. Look at the headlines: "Crime in the City. Murder at Mawson & Williams's. Gigantic Attempted Robbery. Capture of the Criminal." Here, Watson, we are all equally anxious to hear it, so kindly read it aloud to us.'

It appeared from its position in the paper to have been the one event of importance in town, and the account of it ran in this way:

'A desperate attempt at robbery, culminating in the death of one man and the capture of the criminal, occurred this afternoon in the City. For some time back Mawson & Williams, the famous financial house, have been the guardians of securities which amount in the aggregate to a sum of considerably over a million sterling. So conscious was the manager of the responsibility which devolved upon him in consequence of the great interests at stake that safes of the very latest construction have been employed, and an armed watchman has been left day and night in the building. It appears that last week a new clerk named Hall Pycroft was engaged by the firm. This person appears to have been none other than Beddington, the famous forger and cracksman, who, with his brother, has only recently emerged from a five years' spell of penal servitude. By some means, which are not yet clear, he succeeded in winning, under a false name, this official position in the office, which he utilized in order to obtain mouldings of various locks, and a thorough knowledge of the position of the strongroom and the safes.

'It is customary at Mawson's for the clerks to leave at midday on Saturday. Sergeant Tuson, of the City police, was somewhat surprised, therefore, to see a gentleman with a carpet-bag come down the steps at twenty minutes past one. His suspicions being aroused, the sergeant followed the man, and with the aid of Constable Pollock succeeded, after a most desperate resistance, in arresting him. It was at once clear that a daring and gigantic robbery had been committed. Nearly a hundred thousand pounds' worth of American railway bonds, with a large amount of scrip in mines and other companies, was discovered in the bag. On examining the premises the body of the unfortunate watchman was found doubled up and thrust into the largest of the safes, where it would not have been discovered until Monday morning had it not been for the prompt action of Sergeant Tuson. The man's-skull had been shattered by a blow from a poker delivered from behind. There could be no doubt that Beddington had obtained entrance by pretending that he had left something behind him, and having murdered the watchman, rapidly rifled the large safe, and then made off with his booty. His brother, who usually works with him, has not appeared in this job as far as can at present be ascertained, although the police are making energetic inquiries as to his whereabouts.'

'Well, we may save the police some little trouble in that direction,' said Holmes, glancing at the haggard figure huddled up by the window. 'Human nature is a strange mixture, Watson. You see that even a villain and murderer can inspire such affection that his brother turns to suicide when he learns that his neck is forfeited. However, we have no choice as to our action. The doctor and I will remain on guard, Mr Pycroft, if you will have the kindness to step out for the police.'

6

THE ADVENTURE OF
THE CROOKED MAN

One summer night, a few months after my marriage, I was seated by my own hearth smoking a last pipe and nodding over a novel, for my day's work had been an exhausting one. My wife had already gone upstairs, and the sound of the locking of the hall door some time before told me that the servants had also retired. I had risen from my seat and was knocking out the ashes of my pipe when I suddenly heard the clang of the bell.

I looked at the clock. It was a quarter to twelve. This could not be a visitor at so late an hour. A patient evidently, and possibly an all-night sitting. With a wry face I went out into the hall and opened the door. To my astonishment it was Sherlock Holmes who stood upon my step.

'Ah, Watson,' said he, 'I hoped that I might not be too late to catch you.'

'My dear fellow, pray come in.'

'You look surprised, and no wonder! Relieved, too, I fancy! Hum! You still smoke the Arcadia mixture of your bachelor days, then! There's no mistaking that fluffy ash upon your coat. It's easy to tell that you have been accustomed to wear a uniform, Watson. You'll never pass as a pure-bred civilian as long as you keep that habit of carrying your handkerchief in your sleeve. Could you put me up tonight?'

'With pleasure.'

'You told me that you had bachelor quarters for one, and I see that you have no gentleman visitor at present. Your hat-stand proclaims as much.'

'I shall be delighted if you will stay.'

'Thank you. I'll fill the vacant peg then. Sorry to see that you've had the British workman in the house. He's a token of evil. Not the drains, I hope?'

'No, the gas.'

'Ah! He has left two nail-marks from his boot upon your linoleum just where the light strikes it. No, thank you, I had some supper at Waterloo, but I'll smoke a pipe with you with pleasure.'

I handed him my pouch, and he seated himself opposite to me and smoked for some time in silence. I was well aware that nothing but business of importance would have brought him to me at such an hour, so I waited patiently until he should come round to it.

'I see that you are professionally rather busy just now,' said he, glancing very keenly across at me.

'Yes, I've had a busy day,' I answered. 'It may seem very foolish in your eyes,' I added, 'but really I don't know how you deduced it.'

Holmes chuckled to himself.

'I have the advantage of knowing your habits, my dear Watson,' said he. 'When your round is a short one you walk, and when it is a long one you use a hansom. As I perceive that your boots, although used, are by no means dirty, I cannot doubt that you are at present busy enough to justify the hansom.'

'Excellent!' I cried.

'Elementary,' said he. 'It is one of those instances where the reasoner can produce an effect which seems remarkable to his neighbour, because the latter has missed the one little point which is the basis of the deduction. The same may be said, my dear fellow, for the effect of some of these little sketches of yours, which is entirely meretricious, depending as it does upon your retaining in your own hands some factors in the problem which are never imparted to the reader. Now, at present I am in the position of these same readers, for I hold in this hand several threads of one of the strangest cases which ever perplexed a man's brain, and yet I lack the one or two which are needful to complete my theory. But I'll have them, Watson, I'll have them!' His eyes kindled and a slight flush sprang into his thin cheeks. For an instant the veil had lifted upon his keen, intense nature, but for an instant only. When I glanced again his face had resumed that red-Indian composure which had made so many regard him as a machine rather than a man.

'The problem presents features of interest,' said he. 'I may even say exceptional features of interest. I have already looked into the matter, and have come, as I think, within sight of my solution. If you could accompany me in that last step you might be of considerable service to me.'

'I should be delighted.'

'Could you go as far as Aldershot tomorrow?'

'I have no doubt Jackson would take my practice.'

'Very good. I want to start by the 11:10 from Waterloo.'

'That would give me time.'

'Then, if you are not too sleepy, I will give you a sketch of what has happened, and of what remains to be done.'

'I was sleepy before you came. I am quite wakeful now.'

'I will compress the story as far as may be done without omitting anything vital to the case. It is conceivable that you may even have read some account of the matter. It is the supposed murder of Colonel Barclay, of the Royal Munsters, at Aldershot, which I am investigating.'

'I have heard nothing of it.'

'It has not excited much attention yet, except locally. The facts are only two days old. Briefly they are these:

'The Royal Munsters is, as you know, one of the most famous Irish regiments in the British Army. It did wonders both in the Crimea and the Mutiny, and has since that time distinguished itself upon every possible occasion. It was commanded up to Monday night by James Barclay, a gallant veteran, who started as a full private, was raised to commissioned rank for his bravery at the time of the Mutiny, and so lived to command the regiment in which he had once carried a musket.

'Colonel Barclay had married at the time when he was a sergeant, and his wife, whose maiden name was Miss Nancy Devoy, was the daughter of a former colour-sergeant in the same corps. There was, therefore, as can be imagined, some little social friction when the young couple (for they were still young) found themselves in their new surroundings. They appear, however, to have quickly adapted themselves, and Mrs Barclay has always, I understand, been as popular with the ladies of the regiment as her husband was with his brother officers. I may add that she was a woman of great beauty, and that even now, when she has been married for upward of thirty years, she is still of a striking and queenly appearance.

'Colonel Barclay's family life appears to have been a uniformly happy one. Major Murphy, to whom I owe most of my facts, assures me that he has never heard of any misunderstanding between the pair. On the whole, he thinks that Barclay's devotion to his wife was greater than his wife's to Barclay. He was acutely uneasy if he were absent from her for a day. She, on the other hand, though devoted and faithful, was less obtrusively affectionate. But they were regarded in the regiment as the very model of a middle-aged couple. There was absolutely nothing in their mutual relations to prepare people for the tragedy which was to follow.

'Colonel Barclay himself seems to have had some singular

traits in his character. He was a dashing, jovial old soldier in his usual mood, but there were occasions on which he seemed to show himself capable of considerable violence and vindictiveness. This side of his nature, however, appears never to have been turned towards his wife. Another fact which had struck Major Murphy and three out of five of the other officers with whom I conversed was the singular sort of depression which came upon him at times. As the major expressed it, the smile has often been struck from his mouth, as if by some invisible hand, when he has been joining in the gaieties and chaff of the mess-table. For days on end, when the mood was on him, he has been sunk in the deepest gloom. This and a certain tinge of superstition were the only unusual traits in his character which his brother officers had observed. The latter peculiarity took the form of a dislike to being left alone, especially after dark. This puerile feature in a nature which was conspicuously manly had often given rise to comment and conjecture.

'The first battalion of the Royal Munsters (which is the old One Hundred and Seventeenth) has been stationed at Aldershot for some years. The married officers live out of barracks, and the colonel has during all this time occupied a villa called "Lachine," about half a mile from the north camp. The house stands in its own grounds, but the west side of it is not more than thirty yards from the highroad. A coachman and two maids form the staff of servants. These with their master and mistress were the sole occupants of Lachine, for the Barclays had no children, nor was it usual for them to have resident visitors.

'Now for the events at Lachine between nine and ten on the evening of last Monday.

'Mrs Barclay was, it appears, a member of the Roman Catholic Church and had interested herself very much in the establishment of the Guild of St. George, which was formed in connection with the Watt Street Chapel for the purpose of supplying the poor with cast-off clothing. A meeting of the Guild had been held that evening at eight, and Mrs Barclay had hurried over her dinner in order to be present at it. When leaving the house she was heard by the coachman to make some commonplace remark to her husband, and to assure him that she would be back before very long. She then called for Miss Morrison, a young lady who lives in the next villa and the two went off together to their meeting. It lasted forty minutes, and at a quarter past nine Mrs Barclay returned home, having left Miss Morrison at her door as she passed.

'There is a room which is used as a morning-room at Lachine. This faces the road and opens by a large glass folding-door on to the lawn. The lawn is thirty yards across and is only divided from the highway by a low wall with an iron rail above it. It was into this room that Mrs Barclay went upon her return. The blinds were not down, for the room was seldom used in the evening, but Mrs Barclay herself lit the lamp and then rang the bell, asking Jane Stewart, the housemaid, to bring her a cup of tea, which was quite contrary to her usual habits. The colonel had been sitting in the dining-room, but, hearing that his wife had returned, he joined her in the morning-room. The coachman saw him cross the hall and enter it. He was never seen again alive.

'The tea which had been ordered was brought up at the end of ten minutes; but the maid, as she approached the door, was surprised to hear the voices of her master and mistress in furious altercation. She knocked without receiving any answer, and even turned the handle, but only to find that the door was locked upon the inside. Naturally enough she ran down to tell the cook, and the two women with the coachman came up into the hall and listened to the dispute which was still raging. They all agreed that only two voices were to be heard, those of Barclay and of his wife. Barclay's remarks were subdued and abrupt so that none of them were audible to the listeners. The lady's, on the other hand, were most bitter, and when she raised her voice could be plainly heard.

"You coward!" she repeated over and over again. "What can be done now? What can be done now? Give me back my life. I will never so much as breathe the same air with you again! You coward! You coward!" Those were scraps of her conversation, ending in a sudden dreadful cry in the man's voice, with a crash, and a piercing scream from the woman. Convinced that some tragedy had occurred, the coachman rushed to the door and strove to force it, while scream after scream issued from within. He was unable, however, to make his way in, and the maids were too distracted with fear to be of any assistance to him. A sudden thought struck him, however, and he ran through the hall door and round to the lawn upon which the long French windows open. One side of the window was open, which I understand was quite usual in the summertime, and he passed without difficulty into the room. His mistress had ceased to scream and was stretched insensible upon a couch, while with his feet tilted over the side of an armchair, and his head upon the ground near the corner of the fender, was lying the unfortunate soldier stone dead in a pool of his own blood.

'Naturally, the coachman's first thought, on finding that he could do nothing for his master, was to open the door. But here an unexpected and singular difficulty presented itself. The key was not in the inner side of the door, nor could he find it anywhere in the room. He went out again, therefore, through the window, and, having obtained the help of a policeman and of a medical man, he returned. The lady, against whom naturally the strongest suspicion rested, was removed to her room, still in a state of insensibility. The colonel's body was then placed upon the sofa and a careful examination made of the scene of the tragedy.

'The injury from which the unfortunate veteran was suffering was found to be a jagged cut some two inches long at the back part of his head, which had evidently been caused by a violent blow from a blunt weapon. Nor was it difficult to guess what that weapon may have been. Upon the floor, close to the body, was lying a singular club of hard carved wood with a bone handle. The colonel possessed a varied collection of weapons brought from the different countries in which he had fought, and it is conjectured by the police that this club was among his trophies. The servants deny having seen it before, but among the numerous curiosities in the house, it is possible that it may have been overlooked. Nothing else of importance was discovered in the room by the police, save the inexplicable fact that neither upon Mrs Barclay's person nor upon that of the victim nor in any part of the room was the missing key to be found. The door had eventually to be opened by a locksmith from Aldershot.

'That was the state of things, Watson, when upon the Tuesday morning, I, at the request of Major Murphy, went down to Aldershot to supplement the efforts of the police. I think that you will acknowledge that the problem was already one of interest, but my observations soon made me realize that it was in truth much more extraordinary than would at first sight appear.

'Before examining the room I cross-questioned the servants, but only succeeded in eliciting the facts which I have already stated. One other detail of interest was remembered by Jane Stewart, the housemaid. You will remember that on hearing the sound of the quarrel she descended and returned with the other servants. On that first occasion, when she was alone, she says that the voices of her master and mistress were sunk so low that she could hardly hear anything, and judged by their tones rather than their words that they had fallen out. On my pressing her, however, she remembered that she heard the word David uttered twice by the lady. The point is of the utmost importance as guiding us towards the reason of the sudden quarrel. The colonel's name, you remember, was James.

'There was one thing in the case which had made the deepest impression both upon the servants and the police. This was the contortion of the colonel's face. It had set, according to their account, into the most dreadful expression of fear and horror which a human countenance is capable of assuming. More than one person fainted at the mere sight of him, so terrible was the effect. It was quite certain that he had foreseen his fate, and that it had caused him the utmost horror. This, of course, fitted in well enough with the police theory, if the colonel could have seen his wife making a murderous attack upon him. Nor was the fact of the wound being on the back of his head a fatal objection to this, as he might have turned to avoid the blow. No information could be got from the lady herself, who was temporarily insane from an acute attack of brain-fever.

'From the police I learned that Miss Morrison, who you remember went out that evening with Mrs Barclay, denied having any knowledge of what it was which had caused the ill-humour in which her companion had returned.

'Having gathered these facts, Watson, I smoked several pipes over them, trying to separate those which were crucial from others which were merely incidental. There could be no question that the most distinctive and suggestive point in the case was the singular disappearance of the door-key. A most careful search had failed to discover it in the room. Therefore it must have been taken from it. But neither the colonel nor the colonel's wife could have taken it. That was perfectly clear. Therefore a third person must have entered the room. And that third person could only have come in through the window. It seemed to me that a careful examination of the room and the lawn might possibly reveal some traces of this mysterious individual. You know my methods, Watson. There was not one of them which I did not apply to the inquiry. And it ended by my discovering traces, but very different ones from those which I had expected. There had been a man in the room, and he had crossed the lawn coming from the road. I was able to obtain five very clear impressions of his footmarks: one in the roadway itself, at the point where he had climbed the low wall, two on the lawn, and two very faint ones upon the stained boards near the window where he had entered. He had apparently rushed across the lawn, for his toe-marks were much deeper than his heels. But it was not the man who surprised me. It was his companion."

'His companion!'

Holmes pulled a large sheet of tissue-paper out of his pocket and carefully unfolded it upon his knee.

'What do you make of that?' he asked.

The paper was covered with the tracings of the footmarks of some small animal. It had five well-marked footpads, an indication of long nails, and the whole print might be nearly as large as a dessert-spoon.

'It's a dog,' said I.

'Did you ever hear of a dog running up a curtain? I found distinct traces that this creature had done so.'

'A monkey, then?'

'But it is not the print of a monkey.'

'What can it be, then?'

'Neither dog nor cat nor monkey nor any creature that we are familiar with. I have tried to reconstruct it from the measurements. Here are four prints where the beast has been standing motionless. You see that it is no less than fifteen inches from fore-foot to hind. Add to that the length of neck and head, and you get a creature not much less than two feet long—probably more if there is any tail. But now observe this other measurement. The animal has been moving, and we have the length of its stride. In each case it is only about three inches. You have an indication, you see, of a long body with very short legs attached to it. It has not been considerate enough to leave any of its hair behind it. But its general shape must be what I have indicated, and it can run up a curtain, and it is carnivorous.'

'How do you deduce that?'

'Because it ran up the curtain. A canary's cage was hanging

in the window, and its aim seems to have been to get at the bird.'

'Then what was the beast?'

'Ah, if I could give it a name it might go a long way towards solving the case. On the whole, it was probably some creature of the weasel and stoat tribe—and yet it is larger than any of these that I have seen.'

'But what had it to do with the crime?'

'That, also, is still obscure. But we have learned a good deal, you perceive. We know that a man stood in the road looking at the quarrel between the Barclays—the blinds were up and the room lighted. We know, also, that he ran across the lawn, entered the room, accompanied by a strange animal, and that he either struck the colonel or, as is equally possible, that the colonel fell down from sheer fright at the sight of him, and cut his head on the corner of the fender. Finally we have the curious fact that the intruder carried away the key with him when he left.'

'Your discoveries seem to have left the business more obscure than it was before,' said I.

'Quite so. They undoubtedly showed that the affair was much deeper than was at first conjectured. I thought the matter over, and I came to the conclusion that I must approach the case from another aspect. But really, Watson, I am keeping you up, and I might just as well tell you all this on our way to Aldershot tomorrow.'

'Thank you, you have gone rather too far to stop.'

'It is quite certain that when Mrs Barclay left the house at half past seven she was on good terms with her husband. She was never, as I think I have said, ostentatiously affectionate, but she was heard by the coachman chatting with the colonel in a friendly fashion. Now, it was equally certain that, immediately on her return, she had gone to the room in which she was least likely to see her husband, had flown to tea as an agitated woman will, and finally, on his coming in to her, had broken into violent recriminations.

Therefore something had occurred between seven-thirty and nine o'clock which had completely altered her feelings towards him. But Miss Morrison had been with her during the whole of that hour and a half. It was absolutely certain, therefore, in spite of her denial, that she must know something of the matter.

'My first conjecture was that possibly there had been some passages between this young lady and the old soldier, which the former had now confessed to the wife. That would account for the angry return, and also for the girl's denial that anything had occurred. Nor would it be entirely incompatible with most of the words overheard. But there was the reference to David, and there was the known affection of the colonel for his wife to weigh against it, to say nothing of the tragic intrusion of this other man, which might, of course, be entirely disconnected with what had gone before. It was not easy to pick one's steps, but, on the whole, I was inclined to dismiss the idea that there had been anything between the colonel and Miss Morrison, but more than ever convinced that the young lady held the clue as to what it was which had turned Mrs Barclay to hatred of her husband. I took the obvious course, therefore, of calling upon Miss M., of explaining to her that I was perfectly certain that she held the facts in her possession, and of assuring her that her friend, Mrs Barclay, might find herself in the dock upon a capital charge unless the matter were cleared up.

'Miss Morrison is a little ethereal slip of a girl, with timid eyes and blond hair, but I found her by no means wanting in shrewdness and common sense. She sat thinking for some time after I had spoken, and then, turning to me with a brisk air of resolution, she broke into a remarkable statement which I will condense for your benefit.

"I promised my friend that I would say nothing of the matter, and a promise is a promise," said she; "but if I can really help her when so serious a charge is laid against her, and when her own mouth, poor darling, is closed by illness, then I think I am absolved from my promise. I will tell you exactly what happened upon Monday evening.

"We were returning from the Watt Street Mission about a quarter to nine o'clock. On our way we had to pass through Hudson Street, which is a very quiet thoroughfare. There is only one lamp in it, upon the left-hand side, and as we approached this lamp I saw a man coming towards us with his back very bent, and something like a box slung over one of his shoulders. He appeared to be deformed, for he carried his head low and walked with his knees bent. We were passing him when he raised his face to look at us in the circle of light thrown by the lamp, and as he did so he stopped and screamed out in a dreadful voice, 'My God, it's Nancy!' Mrs Barclay turned as white as death and would have fallen down had the dreadful-looking creature not caught hold of her. I was going to call for the police, but she, to my surprise, spoke quite civilly to the fellow.

'I thought you had been dead this thirty years, Henry,' said she in a shaking voice.

'So I have,' said he, and it was awful to hear the tones that he said it in. He had a very dark, fearsome face, and a gleam in his eyes that comes back to me in my dreams. His hair and whiskers were shot with gray, and his face was all crinkled and puckered like a withered apple.

'Just walk on a little way, dear,' said Mrs Barclay; 'I want to have a word with this man. There is nothing to be afraid of.' She tried to speak boldly, but she was still deadly pale and could hardly get her words out for the trembling of her lips.

"'I did as she asked me, and they talked together for a few minutes. Then she came down the street with her eyes blazing, and I saw the crippled wretch standing by the lamp-post and shaking his clenched fists in the air as if he were mad with rage. She never said a word until we were at the door here, when she took me by the hand and begged me to tell no one what had happened.

'It's an old acquaintance of mine who has come down in the world,' said she. When I promised her I would say nothing she kissed me, and I have never seen her since. I have told you now the whole truth, and if I withheld it from the police it is because I did not realize then the danger in which my dear friend stood. I know that it can only be to her advantage that everything should be known."

'There was her statement, Watson, and to me, as you can imagine, it was like a light on a dark night. Everything which had been disconnected before began at once to assume its true place, and I had a shadowy presentiment of the whole sequence of events. My next step obviously was to find the man who had produced such a remarkable impression upon Mrs Barclay. If he were still in Aldershot it should not be a very difficult matter. There are not such a very great number of civilians, and a deformed man was sure to have attracted attention. I spent a day in the search, and by evening—this very evening, Watson—I had run him down. The man's name is Henry Wood, and he lives in lodgings in this same street in which the ladies met him. He has only been five days in the place. In the character of a registration-agent I had a most interesting gossip with his landlady. The man is by trade a conjurer and performer, going round the canteens after nightfall, and giving a little entertainment at each. He carries some creature about with him in that box, about which the landlady seemed to be in considerable trepidation, for she had never seen an animal like it. He uses it in some of his tricks according to her account. So much the woman was able to tell me, and also that it was a wonder the man lived, seeing how twisted he was, and that he spoke in a strange tongue sometimes, and that for the last two nights she had heard him groaning and weeping in his bedroom. He was all right, as far as money went, but in his deposit he had given her what looked like a bad florin. She showed it to me, Watson, and it was an Indian rupee.

'So now, my dear fellow, you see exactly how we stand and why it is I want you. It is perfectly plain that after the ladies parted from this man he followed them at a distance, that he saw the quarrel between husband and wife through the window, that he rushed in, and that the creature which he carried in his box got loose. That is all very certain. But he is the only person in this world who can tell us exactly what happened in that room.'

'And you intend to ask him?'

'Most certainly—but in the presence of a witness.'

'And I am the witness?'

'If you will be so good. If he can clear the matter up, well and good. If he refuses, we have no alternative but to apply for a warrant.'

'But how do you know he'll be there when we return?'

'You may be sure that I took some precautions. I have one of my Baker Street boys mounting guard over him who would stick to him like a burr, go where he might. We shall find him in Hudson Street tomorrow, Watson, and meanwhile I should be the criminal myself if I kept you out of bed any longer.'

It was midday when we found ourselves at the scene of the tragedy, and, under my companion's guidance, we made our way at once to Hudson Street. In spite of his capacity for concealing his emotions, I could easily see that Holmes was in a state of suppressed excitement, while I was myself tingling with that half-sporting, half-intellectual pleasure which I invariably experienced when I associated myself with him in his investigations.

'This is the street,' said he as we turned into a short thoroughfare lined with plain two-storied brick houses. 'Ah, here is Simpson to report.'

'He's in all right, Mr Holmes,' cried a small street Arab, running up to us.

'Good, Simpson!' said Holmes, patting him on the head. 'Come along, Watson. This is the house.' He sent in his card with a message that he had come on important business, and a moment later we were face to face with the man whom we had come to see. In spite of the warm weather he was crouching over a fire, and the little room was like an oven. The man sat all twisted and huddled in his chair in a way which gave an indescribable impression of deformity; but the face which he turned towards us, though worn and swarthy, must at some time have been remarkable for its beauty. He looked suspiciously at us now out of yellow-shot, bilious eyes, and, without speaking or rising, he waved towards two chairs.

'Mr Henry Wood, late of India, I believe,' said Holmes affably. 'I've come over this little matter of Colonel Barclay's death.'

'What should I know about that?'

'That's what I want to ascertain. You know, I suppose, that unless the matter is cleared up, Mrs Barclay, who is an old friend of yours, will in all probability be tried for murder.'

The man gave a violent start.

'I don't know who you are,' he cried, 'nor how you come to know what you do know, but will you swear that this is true that you tell me?'

'Why, they are only waiting for her to come to her senses to arrest her.'

'My God! Are you in the police yourself?'

'No.'

'What business is it of yours, then?'

'It's every man's business to see justice done.'

'You can take my word that she is innocent.'

'Then you are guilty.'

'No, I am not.'

'Who killed Colonel James Barclay, then?'

'"It was a just Providence that killed him. But, mind you this, that if I had knocked his brains out, as it was in my heart to do, he would have had no more than his due from my hands. If his own guilty conscience had not struck him down it is likely enough that I might have had his blood upon my soul. You want me to tell the story. Well, I don't know why I shouldn't, for there's no cause for me to be ashamed of it.

'It was in this way, sir. You see me now with my back like a camel and my ribs all awry, but there was a time when Corporal Henry Wood was the smartest man in the One Hundred and Seventeenth foot. We were in India, then, in cantonments, at a place we'll call Bhurtee. Barclay, who died the other day, was sergeant in the same company as myself, and the belle of the regiment, ay, and the finest girl that ever had the breath of life between her lips, was Nancy Devoy, the daughter of the colour-sergeant. There were two men that loved her, and one that she loved, and you'll smile when you look at this poor thing huddled before the fire and hear me say that it was for my good looks that she loved me.

'Well, though I had her heart, her father was set upon her marrying Barclay. I was a harum-scarum, reckless lad, and he had had an education and was already marked for the sword-belt. But the girl held true to me, and it seemed that I would have had her when the Mutiny broke out, and all hell was loose in the country.

'We were shut up in Bhurtee, the regiment of us with half a battery of artillery, a company of Sikhs, and a lot of civilians and women-folk. There were ten thousand rebels round us, and they were as keen as a set of terriers round a rat-cage. About the second week of it our water gave out, and it was a question whether we could communicate with General Neill's column, which was moving upcountry. It was our only chance, for we could not hope to fight our way out with all the women and children, so I volunteered to go out and to warn General Neill of our danger. My offer was accepted, and I talked it over with Sergeant Barclay, who was supposed to know the ground better than any other man, and who drew up a route by which I might get through the rebel lines. At ten o'clock the same night I started off upon my journey. There were a thousand lives to save, but it was of only one that I was thinking when I dropped over the wall that night.

'My way ran down a dried-up watercourse, which we hoped would screen me from the enemy's sentries; but as I crept round the corner of it I walked right into six of them, who were crouching down in the dark waiting for me. In an instant I was stunned with a blow and bound hand and foot. But the real blow was to my heart and not to my head, for as I came to and listened to as much as I could understand of their talk, I heard enough to tell me that my comrade, the very man who had arranged the way I was to take, had betrayed me by means of a native servant into the hands of the enemy.

'Well, there's no need for me to dwell on that part of it. You know now what James Barclay was capable of. Bhurtee was relieved by Neill next day, but the rebels took me away with them in their retreat, and it was many a long year before ever I saw a white face again. I was tortured and tried to get away, and was captured and tortured again. You can see for yourselves the state in which I was left. Some of them that fled into Nepal took me with them, and then afterwards I was up past Darjeeling. The hill-folk up there murdered the rebels who had me, and I became their slave for a time until I escaped; but instead of going south I had to go north, until I found myself among the Afghans. There I wandered about for many a year, and at last came back to the Punjab, where I lived mostly among the natives and picked up a living by the conjuring tricks that I had learned. What use was it for me, a wretched cripple, to go back to England or to make myself known to my old comrades? Even my wish for revenge would not make me do that. I had rather that Nancy and my old pals should think of Harry Wood as having died with a straight back, than see him living and crawling with a stick like a chimpanzee. They never doubted that I was dead, and I meant that they never should. I heard that Barclay had married Nancy, and that he was rising rapidly in the regiment, but even that did not make me speak.

'But when one gets old one has a longing for home. For years I've been dreaming of the bright green fields and the hedges of England. At last I determined to see them before I died. I saved enough to bring me across, and then I came here where the soldiers are, for I know their ways and how to amuse them and so earn enough to keep me.'

'Your narrative is most interesting,' said Sherlock Holmes. 'I have already heard of your meeting with Mrs Barclay, and your mutual recognition. You then, as I understand, followed her home and saw through the window an altercation between her husband and her, in which she doubtless cast his conduct to you in his teeth. Your own feelings overcame you, and you ran across the lawn and broke in upon them.'

'I did, sir, and at the sight of me he looked as I have never seen a man look before, and over he went with his head on the fender. But he was dead before he fell. I read death on his face as plain as I can read that text over the fire. The bare sight of me was like a bullet through his guilty heart.'

'And then?'

'Then Nancy fainted, and I caught up the key of the door from her hand, intending to unlock it and get help. But as I was doing it it seemed to me better to leave it alone and get away, for the thing might look black against me, and anyway my secret would be out if I were taken. In my haste I thrust the key into my pocket, and dropped my stick while I was chasing Teddy, who had run up the curtain. When I got him into his box, from which he had slipped, I was off as fast as I could run.'

'Who's Teddy?' asked Holmes.

The man leaned over and pulled up the front of a kind of hutch in the corner. In an instant out there slipped a beautiful reddishbrown creature, thin and lithe, with the legs of a stoat, a long, thin nose, and a pair of the finest red eyes that ever I saw in an animal's head.

'It's a mongoose,' I cried.

'Well, some call them that, and some call them ichneumon,' said the man. 'Snake-catcher is what I call them, and Teddy is amazing quick on cobras. I have one here without the fangs, and Teddy catches it every night to please the folk in the canteen."

'Any other point, sir?'

'Well, we may have to apply to you again if Mrs Barclay should prove to be in serious trouble.'

'In that case, of course, I'd come forward.'

'But if not, there is no object in raking up this scandal against a dead man, foully as he has acted. You have at least the satisfaction of knowing that for thirty years of his life his conscience bitterly reproached him for his wicked deed. Ah, there goes Major Murphy on the other side of the street. Good-bye, Wood. I want to learn if anything has happened since yesterday.'

We were in time to overtake the major before he reached the corner.

'Ah, Holmes,' he said, 'I suppose you have heard that all this fuss has come to nothing?'

'What then?'

'The inquest is just over. The medical evidence showed conclusively that death was due to apoplexy. You see it was quite a simple case after all.'

'Oh, remarkably superficial,' said Holmes, smiling. 'Come, Watson, I don't think we shall be wanted in Aldershot any more.'

'There's one thing,' said I as we walked down to the station. 'If the husband's name was James, and the other was Henry, what was this talk about David?'

'That one word, my dear Watson, should have told me the whole story had I been the ideal reasoner which you are so fond of depicting. It was evidently a term of reproach.'

'Of reproach?''

'Yes; David strayed a little occasionally, you know, and on one occasion in the same direction as Sergeant James Barclay. You remember the small affair of Uriah and Bathsheba? My Biblical knowledge is a trifle rusty, I fear, but you will find the story in the first or second of Samuel.'

7

THE ADVENTURE OF THE 'GLORIA SCOTT'

'I have some papers here,' said my friend Sherlock Holmes as we sat one winter's night on either side of the fire, 'which I really think, Watson, that it would be worth your while to glance over. These are the documents in the extraordinary case of the Gloria Scott, and this is the message which struck Justice of the Peace Trevor dead with horror when he read it.'

He had picked from a drawer a little tarnished cylinder, and. undoing the tape, he handed me a short note scrawled upon a half-sheet of slate-gray paper.

"The supply of game for London is going steadily up," it ran. "Head-keeper Hudson, we believe, has been now told to receive all orders for fly-paper and for preservation of your hen-pheasant's life."

As I glanced up from reading this enigmatical message, I saw Holmes chuckling at the expression upon my face.

'You look a little bewildered,' said he.

'I cannot see how such a message as this could inspire horror. It seems to me to be rather grotesque than otherwise.'

'Very likely. Yet the fact remains that the reader, who was a fine, robust old man, was knocked clean down by it as if it had been the butt end of a pistol.'

'You arouse my curiosity,' said I. 'But why did you say just now that there were very particular reasons why I should study this case?'

'Because it was the first in which I was ever engaged.'

I had often endeavoured to elicit from my companion what had first turned his mind in the direction of criminal research, but had never caught him before in a communicative humour. Now he sat forward in his armchair and spread out the documents upon his knees. Then he lit his pipe and sat for some time smoking and turning them over.

'You never heard me talk of Victor Trevor?' he asked. 'He was the only friend I made during the two years I was at college. I was never a very sociable fellow, Watson, always rather fond of moping in my rooms and working out my own little methods of thought, so that I never mixed much with the men of my year. Bar fencing and boxing I had few athletic tastes, and then my line of study was quite distinct from that of the other fellows, so that we had no points of contact at all. Trevor was the only man I knew, and that only through the accident of his bull terrier freezing on to my ankle one morning as I went down to chapel.

'It was a prosaic way of forming a friendship, but it was effective. I was laid by the heels for ten days, and Trevor used to come in to inquire after me. At first it was only a minute's chat but soon his visits lengthened, and before the end of the term we were close friends. He was a hearty, full-blooded fellow, full of spirits and energy, the very opposite to me in most respects, but we had some subjects in common, and it was a bond of union when I found that he was as friendless as I. Finally he invited me down to his father's place at Donnithorpe, in Norfolk, and I accepted his hospitality for a month of the long vacation.

'Old Trevor was evidently a man of some wealth and consideration, a J.P., and a landed proprietor. Donnithorpe is a little hamlet just to the north of Langmere, in the country of the Broads. The house was an old-fashioned, widespread, oak-beamed brick building, with a fine lime-lined avenue leading up to it. There was excellent wild-duck shooting in the fens, remarkably good fishing, a small but select library, taken over, as I understood, from a former occupant, and a tolerable cook, so that he would be a fastidious man who could not put in a pleasant month there.

'Trevor senior was a widower, and my friend his only son.

'There had been a daughter, I heard, but she had died of diphtheria while on a visit to Birmingham. The father interested me extremely. He was a man of little culture, but with a considerable amount of rude strength, both physically and mentally. He knew hardly any books, but he had travelled far, had seen much of the world, and had remembered all that he had learned. In person he was a thick-set, burly man with a shock of grizzled hair, a brown, weather-beaten face, and blue eyes which were keen to the verge of fierceness. Yet he had a reputation for kindness and charity on the countryside, and was noted for the leniency of his sentences from the bench.

'One evening, shortly after my arrival, we were sitting over a glass of port after dinner, when young Trevor began to talk about those habits of observation and inference which I had already formed into a system, although I had not yet appreciated the part which they were to play in my life. The old man evidently thought that his son was exaggerating in his description of one or two trivial feats which I had performed.

'"Come, now, Mr Holmes," said he, laughing good-humouredly. 'I'm an excellent subject, if you can deduce anything from me."

'I fear there is not very much," I answered. "I might suggest that you have gone about in fear of some personal attack within the last twelvemonth."

'The laugh faded from his lips, and he stared at me in great surprise.

"'Well, that's true enough," said he. "You know, Victor," turning to his son, "when we broke up that poaching gang they swore to knife us, and Sir Edward Holly has actually been attacked. I've always been on my guard since then, though I have no idea how you know it."

"You have a very handsome stick," I answered. "By the inscription I observed that you had not had it more than a year. But you have taken some pains to bore the head of it and pour melted lead into the hole so as to make it a formidable weapon. I argued that you would not take such precautions unless you had some danger to fear."

"Anything else?" he asked, smiling.

"You have boxed a good deal in your youth."

"Right again. How did you know it? Is my nose knocked a little out of the straight?"

"'No," said I. "It is your ears. They have the peculiar flattening and thickening which marks the boxing man."

"'Anything else?"

"'You have done a good deal of digging by your callosities."

"'Made all my money at the gold fields."

"'You have been in New Zealand."

"'Right again."

"'You have visited Japan."

"'Quite true."

"'And you have been most intimately associated with someone whose initials were J.A., and whom you afterwards were eager to entirely forget."

'Mr Trevor stood slowly up, fixed his large blue eyes upon me with a strange wild stare, and then pitched forward, with his face among the nutshells which strewed the cloth, in a dead faint.

'You can imagine, Watson, how shocked both his son and I were. His attack did not last long, however, for when we undid his collar and sprinkled the water from one of the finger-glasses over his face, he gave a gasp or two and sat up.

"'Ah, boys,' said he, forcing a smile, "I hope I haven't frightened you. Strong as I look, there is a weak place in my heart, and it does not take much to knock me over. I don't know how you manage this, Mr Holmes, but it seems to me that all the detectives of fact and of fancy would be children in your hands. That's your line of life, sir, and you may take the word of a man who has seen something of the world."

'And that recommendation, with the exaggerated estimate of my ability with which he prefaced it, was, if you will believe me, Watson, the very first thing which ever made me feel that a profession might be made out of what had up to that time been the merest hobby. At the moment, however, I was too much concerned at the sudden illness of my host to think of anything else.

"'I hope that I have said nothing to pain you?' said I.

"'Well, you certainly touched upon rather a tender point. Might I ask how you know, and how much you know?' He spoke now in a half-jesting fashion, but a look of terror still lurked at the back of his eyes.

"'It is simplicity itself,' said I. "When you bared your arm to draw that fish into the boat I saw that J. A. had been tattooed in the bend of the elbow. The letters were still legible, but it was perfectly clear from their blurred appearance, and from the staining of the skin round them, that efforts had been made to obliterate them. It was obvious, then, that those initials had once been very familiar to you, and that you had afterwards wished to forget them."

"'What an eye you have!' he cried with a sigh of relief. "It is just as you say. But we won't talk of it. Of all ghosts the ghosts of our old loves are the worst. Come into the billiard-room and have a quiet cigar.'

'From that day, amid all his cordiality, there was always a touch of suspicion in Mr Trevor's manner towards me. Even his son remarked it. "You've given the governor such a turn," said he, "that he'll never be sure again of what you know and what you don't know." He did not mean to show it, I am sure, but it was so strongly in his mind that it peeped out at every action. At last I became so convinced that I was causing him uneasiness that I drew my visit to a close. On the very day, however, before I left, an incident occurred which proved in the sequel to be of importance.

"We were sitting out upon the lawn on garden chairs, the three of us, basking in the sun and admiring the view across the Broads, when a maid came out to say that there was a man at the door who wanted to see Mr Trevor.

"'What is his name?' asked my host.

"'He would not give any.'

"'What does he want, then?'

"'He says that you know him, and that he only wants a moment's conversation.'

"'Show him round here.' An instant afterwards there appeared a little wizened fellow with a cringing manner and a shambling style of walking. He wore an open jacket, with a splotch of tar on the sleeve, a red-and-black check shirt, dungaree trousers, and heavy boots badly worn. His face was thin and brown and crafty, with a perpetual smile upon it, which showed an irregular line of yellow teeth, and his crinkled hands were half closed in a way that is distinctive of sailors. As he came slouching across the lawn I heard Mr Trevor make a sort of hiccoughing noise in his throat, and, jumping out of his chair, he ran into the house. He was back in a moment, and I smelt a strong reek of brandy as he passed me.

"'Well, my man,' said he. 'What can I do for you?'

'The sailor stood looking at him with puckered eyes, and with the same loose-lipped smile upon his face.

"'You don't know me?' he asked.

"'Why, dear me, it is surely Hudson,' said Mr Trevor in a tone of surprise.

"Hudson it is, sir," said the seaman. "Why, it's thirty year and more since I saw you last. Here you are in your house, and me still picking my salt meat out of the harness cask."

"'Tut, you will find that I have not forgotten old times," cried Mr Trevor, and, walking towards the sailor, he said something in a low voice. "Go into the kitchen," he continued out loud, "and you will get food and drink. I have no doubt that I shall find you a situation."

"Thank you, sir," said the seaman, touching his forelock. "I'm just off a two-yearer in an eight-knot tramp, short-handed at that, and I wants a rest. I thought I'd get it either with Mr Beddoes or with you."

"'Ah!" cried Mr Trevor. "You know where Mr Beddoes is?"

"'Bless you, sir, I know where all my old friends are," said the fellow with a sinister smile, and he slouched off after the maid to the kitchen. Mr Trevor mumbled something to us about having been shipmate with the man when he was going back to the diggings, and then, leaving us on the lawn, he went indoors. An hour later, when we entered the house, we found him stretched dead drunk upon the dining-room sofa. The whole incident left a most ugly impression upon my mind, and I was not sorry next day to leave Donnithorpe behind me, for I felt that my presence must be a source of embarrassment to my friend.

'All this occurred during the first month of the long vacation. I went up to my London rooms, where I spent seven weeks working out a few experiments in organic chemistry. One day, however, when the autumn was far advanced and the vacation drawing to a close, I received a telegram from my friend imploring me to return to Donnithorpe, and saying that he was in great need of my advice and assistance. Of course I dropped everything and set out for the North once more.

'He met me with the dog-cart at the station, and I saw at a glance that the last two months had been very trying ones for him.

He had grown thin and careworn, and had lost the loud, cheery manner for which he had been remarkable.

'"The governor is dying," were the first words he said.

'"Impossible!" I cried. "What is the matter?"

'"Apoplexy. Nervous shock. He's been on the verge all day. I doubt if we shall find him alive."

'I was, as you may think, Watson, horrified at this unexpected news.

'"What has caused it?" I asked.

'"Ah, that is the point. Jump in and we can talk it over while we drive. You remember that fellow who came upon the evening before you left us?"

'"Perfectly."

'"Do you know who it was that we let into the house that day?"

'"I have no idea."

'"It was the devil, Holmes," he cried.

'I stared at him in astonishment.

'"Yes, it was the devil himself. We have not had a peaceful hour since—not one. The governor has never held up his head from that evening, and now the life has been crushed out of him and his heart broken, all through this accursed Hudson."

'"What power had he, then?"

'"Ah, that is what I would give so much to know. The kindly, charitable good old governor—how could he have fallen into the clutches of such a ruffian! But I am so glad that you have come, Holmes. I trust very much to your judgment and discretion, and I know that you will advise me for the best."

'We were dashing along the smooth white country road, with the long stretch of the Broads in front of us glimmering in the red light of the setting sun. From a grove upon our left I could already see the high chimneys and the flagstaff which marked the squire's dwelling.

"'My father made the fellow gardener," said my companion, "and then, as that did not satisfy him, he was promoted to be butler. The house seemed to be at his mercy, and he wandered about and did what he chose in it. The maids complained of his drunken habits and his vile language. The dad raised their wages all round to recompense them for the annoyance. The fellow would take the boat and my father's best gun and treat himself to little shooting trips. And all this with such a sneering, leering, insolent face that I would have knocked him down twenty times over if he had been a man of my own age. I tell you, Holmes, I have had to keep a tight hold upon myself all this time and now I am asking myself whether, if I had let myself go a little more, I might not have been a wiser man.

"Well, matters went from bad to worse with us, and this animal Hudson became more and more intrusive, until at last, on his making some insolent reply to my father in my presence one day, I took him by the shoulders and turned him out of the room. He slunk away with a livid face and two venomous eyes which uttered more threats than his tongue could do. I don't know what passed between the poor dad and him after that, but the dad came to me next day and asked me whether I would mind apologizing to Hudson. I refused, as you can imagine, and asked my father how he could allow such a wretch to take such liberties with himself and his household.

'Ah, my boy,' said he, 'it is all very well to talk, but you don't know how I am placed. But you shall know, Victor. I'll see that you shall know, come what may. You wouldn't believe harm of your poor old father, would you, lad?' He was very much moved and shut himself up in the study all day, where I could see through the window that he was writing busily.

'That evening there came what seemed to me to be a grand release, for Hudson told us that he was going to leave us. He walked into the dining-room as we sat after dinner and announced his intention in the thick voice of a half-drunken man.

'I've had enough of Norfolk,' said he. 'I'll run down to Mr Beddoes in Hampshire. He'll be as glad to see me as you were, I daresay.'

'You're not going away in an unkind spirit, Hudson, I hope,' said my father with a tameness which made my blood boil.

'I've not had my, pology,' said he sulkily, glancing in my direction.

'Victor, you will acknowledge that you have used this worthy fellow rather roughly,' said the dad, turning to me.

'On the contrary, I think that we have both shown extraordinary patience towards him,' I answered.

'Oh, you do, do you?' he snarled. 'Very good, mate. We'll see about that!'

"He slouched out of the room and half an hour afterwards left the house, leaving my father in a state of pitiable nervousness. Night after night I heard him pacing his room, and it was just as he was recovering his confidence that the blow did at last fall.'

"'And how?" I asked eagerly.

"'In a most extraordinary fashion. A letter arrived for my father yesterday evening, bearing the Fordingham postmark. My father read it, clapped both his hands to his head, and began running round the room in little circles like a man who has been driven out of his senses. When I at last drew him down on to the sofa, his mouth and eyelids were all puckered on one side, and I saw that he had a stroke. Dr. Fordham came over at once. We put him to bed, but the paralysis has spread, he has shown no sign of returning consciousness, and I think that we shall hardly find him alive."

"'You horrify me, Trevor!" I cried. "What then could have been in this letter to cause so dreadful a result?"

"'Nothing. There lies the inexplicable part of it. The message was absurd and trivial. Ah, my God, it is as I feared!"

'As he spoke we came round the curve of the avenue and saw

in the fading light that every blind in the house had been drawn down. As we dashed up to the door, my friend's face convulsed with grief, a gentleman in black emerged from it.

"'When did it happen, doctor?" asked Trevor.

"'Almost immediately after you left."

"'Did he recover consciousness?"

"'For an instant before the end."

"'Any message for me?"

"'Only that the papers were in the back drawer of the Japanese cabinet."

'My friend ascended with the doctor to the chamber of death while I remained in the study, turning the whole matter over and over in my head, and feeling as sombre as ever I had done in my life. What was the past of this Trevor, pugilist, traveller, and gold-digger, and how had he placed himself in the power of this acid-faced seaman? Why, too, should he faint at an allusion to the half-effaced initials upon his arm and die of fright when he had a letter from Fordingham? Then I remembered that Fordingham was in Hampshire, and that this Mr Beddoes, whom the seaman had gone to visit and presumably to blackmail, had also been mentioned as living in Hampshire. The letter, then, might either come from Hudson, the seaman, saying that he had betrayed the guilty secret which appeared to exist, or it might come from Beddoes, warning an old confederate that such a betrayal was imminent. So far it seemed clear enough. But then how could this letter be trivial and grotesque, as described by the son? He must have misread it. If so, it must have been one of those ingenious secret codes which mean one thing while they seem to mean another. I must see this letter. If there was a hidden meaning in it, I was confident that I could pluck it forth. For an hour I sat pondering over it in the gloom, until at last a weeping maid brought in a lamp, and close at her heels came my friend Trevor, pale but composed, with these very papers which lie upon my knee held in his grasp. He sat down opposite to me, drew the lamp to the edge of the table, and handed me a short note scribbled, as you see, upon a single sheet of gray paper. "The supply of game for London is going steadily up," it ran. "Head-keeper Hudson, we believe, has been now told to receive all orders for fly-paper and for preservation of your hen-pheasant's life."

'I daresay my face looked as bewildered as yours did just now when first I read this message. Then I reread it very carefully. It was evidently as I had thought, and some secret meaning must lie buried in this strange combination of words. Or could it be that there was a prearranged significance to such phrases as "fly-paper" and "hen-pheasant"? Such a meaning would be arbitrary and could not be deduced in any way. And yet I was loath to believe that this was the case, and the presence of the word Hudson seemed to show that the subject of the message was as I had guessed, and that it was from Beddoes rather than the sailor. I tried it backward, but the combination 'life pheasant's hen' was not encouraging. Then I tried alternate words, but neither 'the of for' nor 'supply game London' promised to throw any light upon it.

'And then in an instant the key of the riddle was in my hands, and I saw that every third word, beginning with the first, would give a message which might well drive old Trevor to despair.

'It was short and terse, the warning, as I now read it to my companion:

'"The game is up. Hudson has told all. Fly for your life."

'Victor Trevor sank his face into his shaking hands. "It must be that, I suppose," said he. "This is worse than death, for it means disgrace as well. But what is the meaning of these 'headkeepers' and 'hen-pheasants'?"

"It means nothing to the message, but it might mean a good deal to us if we had no other means of discovering the sender. You see that he has begun by writing 'The...game...is,' and so on. Afterwards he had, to fulfil the prearranged cipher, to fill in any two words in each space. He would naturally use the first words which came to his mind, and if there were so many which referred to sport among them, you may be tolerably sure that he is either an ardent shot or interested in breeding. Do you know anything of this Beddoes?"

"'Why, now that you mention it," said he, "I remember that my poor father used to have an invitation from him to shoot over his preserves every autumn."

"'Then it is undoubtedly from him that the note comes," said I. "It only remains for us to find out what this secret was which the sailor Hudson seems to have held over the heads of these two wealthy and respected men."

"'Alas, Holmes, I fear that it is one of sin and shame!" cried my friend. "But from you I shall have no secrets. Here is the statement which was drawn up by my father when he knew that the danger from Hudson had become imminent. I found it in the Japanese cabinet, as he told the doctor. Take it and read it to me, for I have neither the strength nor the courage to do it myself."

'These are the very papers, Watson, which he handed to me, and I will read them to you, as I read them in the old study that night to him. They are endorsed outside, as you see, "Some particulars of the voyage of the bark Gloria Scott, from her leaving Falmouth on the 8th October, 1855, to her destruction in N. Lat. 15 degrees 20'. W. Long. 25 degrees 14', on Nov. 6th." It is in the form of a letter, and runs in this way:

"'My dear, dear son, now that approaching disgrace begins to darken the closing years of my life, I can write with all truth and honesty that it is not the terror of the law, it is not the loss of my position in the county, nor is it my fall in the eyes of all who have known me, which cuts me to the heart; but it is the thought that you should come to blush for me—you who love me and who have seldom, I hope, had reason to do other than respect me. But if the blow falls which is forever hanging over me, then I should wish you to read this, that you may know straight from me how far I have been to blame. On the other hand, if all should go well (which may kind God Almighty grant!), then, if by any chance this paper should be still undestroyed and should fall into your hands, I conjure you, by all you hold sacred, by the memory of your dear mother, and by the love which has been between us, to hurl it into the fire and to never give one thought to it again.

"If then your eye goes on to read this line, I know that I shall already have been exposed and dragged from my home, or, as is more likely, for you know that my heart is weak, be lying with my tongue sealed forever in death. In either case the time for suppression is past, and every word which I tell you is the naked truth, and this I swear as I hope for mercy.

"My name, dear lad, is not Trevor. I was James Armitage in my younger days, and you can understand now the shock that it was to me a few weeks ago when your college friend addressed me in words which seemed to imply that he had surprised my secret. As Armitage it was that I entered a London banking-house, and as Armitage I was convicted of breaking my country's laws, and was sentenced to transportation. Do not think very harshly of me, laddie. It was a debt of honour, so called, which I had to pay, and I used money which was not my own to do it, in the certainty that I could replace it before there could be any possibility of its being missed. But the most dreadful ill-luck pursued me. The money which I had reckoned upon never came to hand, and a premature examination of accounts exposed my deficit. The case might have been dealt leniently with, but the laws were more harshly administered thirty years ago than now, and on my twenty-third birthday I found myself chained as a felon with thirty-seven other convicts in 'tween-decks of the bark Gloria Scott, bound for Australia.

"It was the year '55, when the Crimean War was at its height, and the old convict ships had been largely used as transports in the Black Sea. The government was compelled, therefore, to use smaller and less suitable vessels for sending out their prisoners. The Gloria Scott had been in the Chinese tea-trade, but she was an old-fashioned, heavy-bowed, broad-beamed craft, and the new clippers had cut her out. She was a five-hundred-ton boat; and besides her thirty-eight jail-birds, she carried twenty-six of a crew, eighteen soldiers, a captain, three mates, a doctor, a chaplain, and four warders. Nearly a hundred souls were in her, all told, when we set sail from Faltnouth.

"The partitions between the cells of the convicts, instead of being of thick oak, as is usual in convict-ships, were quite thin and frail. The man next to me, upon the aft side, was one whom I had particularly noticed when we were led down the quay. He was a young man with a clear, hairless face, a long, thin nose, and rather nut-cracker jaws. He carried his head very jauntily in the air, had a swaggering style of walking, and was above all else, remarkable for his extraordinary height. I don't think any of our heads would have come up to his shoulder, and I am sure that he could not have measured less than six and a half feet. It was strange among so many sad and weary faces to see one which was full of energy and resolution. The sight of it was to me like a fire in a snowstorm. I was glad, then, to find that he was my neighbour, and gladder still when, in the dead of the night, I heard a whisper close to my ear and found that he had managed to cut an opening in the board which separated us.

'Hullo, chummy!' said he, 'what's your name, and what are you here for?'

"'I answered him, and asked in turn who I was talking with.

'I'm Jack Prendergast,' said he, 'and by God! You'll learn to bless my name before you've done with me.'

"I remembered hearing of his case, for it was one which had made an immense sensation throughout the country some time before my own arrest. He was a man of good family and of great ability, but of incurably vicious habits, who had by an ingenious system of fraud obtained huge sums of money from the leading London merchants.

'Ha, ha! You remember my case!' said he proudly.

'Very well, indeed.'

'Then maybe you remember something queer about it?'

'"What was that, then?"'

'I'd had nearly a quarter of a million, hadn't I?'

'So it was said.'

'But none was recovered, eh?'

'No.'

'Well, where d'ye suppose the balance is?' he asked.

'I have no idea,' said I.

'Right between my finger and thumb,' he cried. 'By God! I've got mare pounds to my name than you've hairs on your head. And if you've money, my son, and know how to handle it and spread it, you can do anything. Now, you don't think it likely that a man who could do anything is going to wear his breeches out sitting in the stinking hold of a rat-gutted beetle-ridden, mouldy old coffin of a Chin China coaster. No, sir, such a man will look after himself and will look after his chums. You may lay to that! You hold on to him, and you may kiss the book that he'll haul you through.'

"That was his style of talk, and at first I thought it meant nothing; but after a while, when he had tested me and sworn me in with all possible solemnity, he let me understand that there really was a plot to gain command of the vessel. A dozen of the prisoners had hatched it before they came aboard, Prendergast was the leader, and his money was the motive power.

'I'd a partner,' said he, 'a rare good man, as true as a stock to a barrel. He's got the dibbs, he has, and where do you think he is at this moment? Why, he's the chaplain of this ship—the chaplain, no less! He came aboard with a black coat, and his papers right, and money enough in his box to buy the thing right up from keel to main-truck. The crew are his, body and soul. He could buy 'em at so much a gross with a cash discount, and he did it before ever they signed on. He's got two of the warders and Mereer, the second mate, and he'd get the captain himself, if he thought him worth it.'

'What are we to do, then?' I asked.

'What do you think?' said he. 'We'll make the coats of some of these soldiers redder than ever the tailor did.'

'But they are armed,' said I.

'And so shall we be, my boy. There's a brace of pistols for every mother's son of us; and if we can't carry this ship, with the crew at our back, it's time we were all sent to a young misses' boarding-school. You speak to your mate upon the left tonight, and see if he is to be trusted.'

"I did so and found my other neighbour to be a young fellow in much the same position as myself, whose crime had been forgery. His name was Evans, but he afterwards changed it, like myself, and he is now a rich and prosperous man in the south of England. He was ready enough to join the conspiracy, as the only means of saving ourselves, and before we had crossed the bay there were only two of the prisoners who were not in the secret. One of these was of weak mind, and we did not dare to trust him, and the other was suffering from jaundice and could not be of any use to us.

"From the beginning there was really nothing to prevent us from taking possession of the ship. The crew were a set of ruffians, specially picked for the job. The sham chaplain came into our cells to exhort us, carrying a black bag, supposed to be full of tracts, and so often did he come that by the third day we had each stowed away at the foot of our beds a file, a brace of pistols, a pound of powder, and twenty slugs. Two of the warders were agents of Prendergast, and the second mate was his right-hand man. The captain, the two mates, two warders, Lieutenant Martin, his eighteen soldiers, and the doctor were all that we had against us. Yet, safe as it was, we determined to neglect no precaution, and to make our attack suddenly by night. It came, however, more quickly than we expected, and in this way.

"'One evening, about the third week after our start, the doctor had come down to see one of the prisoners who was ill, and putting his hand down on the bottom of his bunk, he felt the outline of the pistols. If he had been silent he might have blown the whole thing, but he was a nervous little chap, so he gave a cry of surprise and turned so pale that the man knew what was up in an instant and seized him. He was gagged before he could give the alarm and tied down upon the bed. He had unlocked the door that led to the deck, and we were through it in a rush. The two sentries were shot down, and so was a corporal who came running to see what was the matter. There were two more soldiers at the door of the stateroom, and their muskets seemed not to be loaded, for they never fired upon us, and they were shot while trying to fix their bayonets. Then we rushed on into the Captain's cabin, but as we pushed open the door there was an explosion from within, and there he lay with his brains smeared over the chart of the Atlantic which was pinned upon the table, while the chaplain stood with a smoking pistol in his hand at his elbow. The two mates had both been seized by the crew, and the whole business seemed to be settled.

"The stateroom was next the cabin, and we flocked in there and flopped down on the settees, all speaking together, for we were just mad with the feeling that we were free once more. There were lockers all round, and Wilson, the sham chaplain, knocked one of them in, and pulled out a dozen of brown sherry. We cracked off the necks of the bottles, poured the stuff out into tumblers, and were just tossing them off when in an instant without warning there came the roar of muskets in our ears, and the saloon was so full of smoke that we could not see across the table. When it cleared again the place was a shambles. Wilson and eight others were wriggling on the top of each other on the floor, and the blood and the brown sherry on that table turn me sick now when I think of it. We were so cowed by the sight that I think we should have given the job up if it had not been for Prendergast. He bellowed like a bull and rushed for the door with all that were left alive at his heels. Out we ran, and there on the poop were the lieutenant and ten of his men. The swing skylights above the saloon table had been a bit open, and they had fired on us through the slit. We got on them before they could load, and they stood to it like men; but we had the upper hand of them, and in five minutes it was all over. My God! Was there ever a slaughter-house like that ship! Prendergast was like a raging devil, and he picked the soldiers up as if they had been children and threw them overboard alive or dead. There was one sergeant that was horribly wounded and yet kept on swimming for a surprising time until someone in mercy blew out his brains. When the fighting was over there was no one left of our enemies except just the warders, the mates, and the doctor.

"It was over them that the great quarrel arose. There were many of us who were glad enough to win back our freedom, and yet who had no wish to have murder on our souls. It was one thing to knock the soldiers over with their muskets in their hands, and it was another to stand by while men were being killed in cold blood. Eight of us, five convicts and three sailors, said that we would not see it done. But there was no moving Prendergast and those who were with him. Our only chance of safety lay in making a clean job of it, said he, and he would not leave a tongue with power to wag in a witness-box. It nearly came to our sharing the fate of the prisoners, but at last he said that if we wished we might take a boat and go. We jumped at the offer, for we were already sick of these bloodthirsty doings, and we saw that there would be worse before it was done. We were given a suit of sailor togs each, a barrel of water, two casks, one of junk and one of biscuits, and a compass. Prendergast threw us over a chart, told us that we were shiprecked mariners whose ship had foundered in Lat. 15 degrees and Long. 25 degrees west, and then cut the painter and let us go.

"And now I come to the most surprising part of my story, my dear son. The seamen had hauled the fore-yard aback during the rising, but now as we left them they brought it square again, and as there was a light wind from the north and east the bark began to draw slowly away from us. Our boat lay, rising and falling, upon the long, smooth rollers, and Evans and I, who were the most educated of the party, were sitting in the sheets working out our position and planning what coast we should make for. It was a nice question, for the Cape Verdes were about five hundred miles to the north of us, and the African coast about seven hundred to the east. On the whole, as the wind was coming round to the north, we thought that Sierra Leone might be best and turned our head in that direction, the bark being at that time nearly hull down on our starboard quarter. Suddenly as we looked at her we saw a dense black cloud of smoke shoot up from her, which hung like a monstrous tree upon the sky line. A few seconds later a roar like thunder burst upon our ears, and as the smoke thinned away there was no sign left of the Gloria Scott. In an instant we swept the boat's head round again and pulled with all our strength for the place where the haze still trailing over the water marked the scene of this catastrophe.

"It was a long hour before we reached it, and at first we feared that we had come too late to save anyone. A splintered boat and a number of crates and fragments of spars rising and falling on the waves showed us where the vessel had foundered; but there was no sign of life, and we had turned away in despair, when we heard a cry for help and saw at some distance a piece of wreckage with a man lying stretched across it. When we pulled him aboard the boat he proved to be a young seaman of the name of Hudson, who was so burned and exhausted that he could give us no account of what had happened until the following morning.

"It seemed that after we had left, Prendergast and his gang had proceeded to put to death the five remaining prisoners. The two warders had been shot and thrown overboard, and so also had the third mate. Prendergast then descended into the 'tweendecks and with his own hands cut the throat of the unfortunate surgeon. There only remained the first mate, who was a bold and active man. When he saw the convict approaching him with the bloody knife in his hand he kicked off his bonds, which he had somehow contrived to loosen, and rushing down the deck he plunged into the after-hold. A dozen convicts, who descended with their pistols in search of him, found him with a match-box in his hand seated beside an open powder-barrel, which was one of the hundred carried on board, and swearing that he would blow all hands up if he were in any way molested. An instant later the explosion occurred, though Hudson thought it was caused by the misdirected bullet of one of the convicts rather than the mate's match. Be the cause what it may, it was the end of the Gloria Scott and of the rabble who held command of her.

"Such, in a few words, my dear boy, is the history of this terrible business in which I was involved. Next day we were picked up by the brig Hotspur, bound for Australia, whose captain found no difficulty in believing that we were the survivors of a passenger ship which had foundered. The transport ship Gloria Scott was set down by the Admiralty as being lost at sea, and no word has ever leaked out as to her true fate. After an excellent voyage the Hotspur landed us at Sydney, where Evans and I changed our names and made our way to the diggings, where, among the crowds who were gathered from all nations, we had no difficulty in losing our former identities. The rest I need not relate. We prospered, we travelled, we came back as rich colonials to England, and we bought country estates. For more than twenty years we have led peaceful and useful lives, and we hoped that our past was forever buried. Imagine, then, my feelings when in the seaman who came to us I recognized instantly the man who had been picked off the wreck. He had tracked us down somehow and had set himself to live upon our fears. You will understand now how it was that I strove to keep the peace with him, and you will in some measure sympathize with me in the fears which fill me, now that he has gone from me to his other victim with threats upon his tongue."'

'Underneath is written in a hand so shaky as to be hardly legible, "Beddoes writes in cipher to say H. has told all. Sweet Lord, have mercy on our souls!"'

'That was the narrative which I read that night to young Trevor, and I think, Watson, that under the circumstances it was a dramatic one. The good fellow was heart-broken at it, and went out to the Terai tea planting, where I hear that he is doing well. As to the sailor and Beddoes, neither of them was ever heard of again after that day on which the letter of warning was written. They both disappeared utterly and completely. No complaint had been lodged with the police, so that Beddoes had mistaken a threat for a deed. Hudson had been seen lurking about, and it was believed by the police that he had done away with Beddoes and had fled. For myself I believe that the truth was exactly the opposite. I think that it is most probable that Beddoes, pushed to desperation and believing himself to have been already betrayed, had revenged himself upon Hudson, and had fled from the country with as much money as he could lay his hands on. Those are the facts of the case, Doctor, and if they are of any use to your collection, I am sure that they are very heartily at your service.'

ABOUT TERRY O'BRIEN

Terry O'Brien is an academic with three decades of experience in teaching language and communication skills in India and abroad. He also headed a college under the auspices of the University of Delhi.

A prolific writer, with several books to his credit, Terry O'Brien is a reputed professional motivational speaker and a quizmaster.